Memories of The Highland Trilogy

THE LOCH'S LULLABY

Book 2

By Morgan DeSpiegelaere

Disclaimer

This is a work of fiction. All characters, places, and events depicted in this novel are products of the author's imagination. Any resemblance to real persons, living or dead, or actual events is purely coincidental. The locations, names, and circumstances within this story have been crafted for the sole purpose of the narrative and are not based on real-world counterpart

Dedication

To those who believe in the magic of the universe, the power of love, and the what guides us forward. This story is for you, for those who find beauty in the untold and strength in the unknown.

And to the dreamers — may you always chase the shadows of your heart

Acknowledgments

To my family and friends — thank you for your endless support, encouragement, and belief in my stories, even on the days when doubt crept in. Your love and patience fuel my passion to write.

To my readers — your love of stories, your connection to these characters, and your unwavering support mean more to me than words can express. This book exists because of you, and I'm endlessly grateful for your kind hearts and your trust in my work.

And finally, to my dreams — the ones that keep me awake at night, pushing me to tell stories that linger in the hearts of others. You are my guiding stars.

Prologue

The night was heavy with mist, clinging to the air like a ghost's embrace. The surface of the loch lay still, black as ink, reflecting the sliver of a waning moon. A woman stood at the water's edge, her breath rising in shallow gasps, her cloak heavy with the weight of her grief. The Highlands had always been her home, but now, they felt like a graveyard of memories she could no longer bear.

Her love was gone—stolen from her by the cruelty of fate, by the hand of another. A fisherman, strong and kind, with eyes that mirrored the loch at dawn. He had whispered promises against her skin, vows of a future they were never meant to have. The man she was meant to wed had seen to that. And now, his blood stained the shores she once walked with joy.

She staggered forward, the wind howling through the glen like the wail of a mourning mother. The villagers would say she was mad. That grief had unraveled her mind. But she knew the truth—her heart had shattered the moment he was taken from her. There was nothing left.

Tilting her head to the sky, she let out a cry, raw and broken, before her voice softened into a song—a lullaby once sung in whispers between lovers, now an offering to the loch. Her voice wove through the night, a melody carried by the wind, a lament of sorrow and longing. She sang for him, for the love they lost, for the life they would never share.

The water stirred. A ripple. A whisper.

She stepped forward, the icy depths curling around her ankles, then her knees. The loch called to her, and she answered. Deeper. Deeper still, until the mist swallowed her whole. The song faded, swallowed by the night, leaving nothing but silence in its wake.

They never found her body.

But some say, when the mist rolls in and the loch is still, you can hear the melody drifting over the water — the lullaby of a love lost to the depths, waiting to be heard once more.

Chapter 1: The Road to Ruin Bay

The Highlands rose before her, wreathed in mist and memory, their jagged peaks carving into a sky the color of slate. Isla Rowan pressed her forehead to the cool glass of the bus window, her breath fogging against the reflection of her own tired blue eyes, and her long curly dark red hair cascading everywhere. The winding road twisted through the hills, cutting through valleys where the land stretched endlessly in shades of green and gold, a beauty both untamed and sorrowful. It felt right. It felt like somewhere a heart could heal—if such a thing was even possible.

She had left Ireland behind with nothing but a single suitcase and a heart too heavy to carry. Her mother was gone, taken by an illness that ravaged faster than anyone had prepared for. And then there was the man who had promised forever, only to rip it from her hands before it had the chance to bloom. Isla had loved him, foolishly, wholly. And when he left, she felt the loss like a wound that would never close.

So she did what artists did when the world became too sharp, too unbearable—she ran to find solitude in beauty, seeking inspiration in places untouched by the weight of modern life. She had read about the village of Ruin Bay in a tattered book tucked away in a Dublin bookshop, and something had called to her then, just as it did now. A forgotten village nestled against a great loch, rumored to be as haunted as it was breathtaking. Perfect.

The bus shuddered to a stop, and the driver cast a glance at her in the rearview mirror. "Last stop, lass. Ruin Bay."

She pulled her coat tight around her shoulders as she stepped off the bus, the air thick with damp earth and the sharp scent of pine. The village was smaller than she had expected, tucked against the water's edge with stone cottages hunched beneath the weight of time. The loch stretched before her, dark and endless, its surface rippling under the touch of the wind.

Isla inhaled deeply, as though she could breathe in the history here, the stories buried beneath moss and stone. The locals watched her from their doorways, their eyes lingering just a little too long before they returned to whatever task she had interrupted. Strangers weren't common here.

She set her bag down for a moment, stretching her fingers against the chill. That was when she heard it.

A sound so faint it could have been the wind through the trees. A melody, low and sorrowful, drifting over the water.

She turned sharply, her pulse quickening. The loch was silent now, as though it had swallowed the sound whole.

A voice behind her broke the spell. "Ye best stay away from the water at night."

Isla turned to find an elderly woman watching her from the threshold of a weathered cottage. Her face was lined, her hands worn by years of work. "Why?" Isla asked.

The woman's gaze flickered to the loch and then back to Isla. "Because the loch remembers. And it sings for those who listen."

Isla swallowed against the chill creeping up her spine. She had come here to escape ghosts, but it seemed Ruin Bay had plenty of its own.

Chapter 2: Whispers on The Wind

The wind had a bite to it, sharp and salty from the loch, as Isla pulled her coat tighter around herself. Ruin Bay was unlike anywhere she had ever been. The village was nestled against the water, its stone cottages hunched like old men against the cold, their roofs darkened with age and sea spray. The air carried the scent of damp earth,

wood smoke, and something wilder —
something she couldn't quite name.

She had arrived late the previous
evening. By the time she reached the
tiny cottage she had rented,
exhaustion had settled into her bones,
and sleep had claimed her before she
could even properly take in her
surroundings.

Now, in the morning light, Ruin
Bay revealed itself in muted shades of
grey and green, the loch stretching out
like a liquid mirror, rippling only
when the wind sighed across its
surface. It was hauntingly beautiful,
and yet, there was a weight in the air,
an unspoken hush that made her
uneasy.

She made her way toward the
village center, a cluster of small shops
and a lone pub, The Black Harp,
which stood at the edge of the water.
The sign creaked on its rusted hinge as
she pushed the door open, stepping

into the warmth of flickering lanterns and the scent of peat smoke curling through the air.

A few heads turned, assessing her with quiet curiosity. Strangers were rare here — she knew that much from the sparse information she'd found online. The bartender, a stout woman with a no-nonsense expression, raised an eyebrow.

"Morning, lass. New to Ruin Bay?"

Isla nodded, slipping onto a stool. "Yes, just arrived yesterday. I'm renting the old Rowan cottage."

A silence fell over the small group of patrons. A man sitting near the fire — a fisherman, judging by his weathered face and thick woolen sweater — exchanged glances with another. The bartender exhaled through her nose, setting a cup of tea in front of Isla.

"A fine place," she said at last, though there was something guarded in her tone. "A bit far from the village, though."

Isla wrapped her hands around the warm ceramic. "That's what I wanted. Somewhere quiet."

A snort came from the older fisherman. "Quiet's one word for it. Isolated's another."

The bartender shot him a look before turning back to Isla. "You're an artist, then?"

Isla nodded. "A painter. I needed some time away."

A murmur of understanding rippled through them. Artists were known to seek solace in places like this. But there was something else beneath their acknowledgment — something they weren't saying.

"You'll want to mind yourself near the loch at night," the bartender said after a moment. "The water carries strange sounds, and the mist can play tricks on you."

Isla frowned. "Strange sounds?"

The older fisherman tapped his knuckles against the wooden table. "They call it the Loch's Lullaby. An old tale. Some say the loch sings when the mist rolls in. A song to call the lost."

A shiver ran down Isla's spine, but she forced a smile. "That sounds like something out of a ghost story."

The bartender's gaze held hers, steady and knowing. "Aye, and some stories are best left alone."

Isla took a slow sip of her tea, letting the warmth spread through her. She had come here to heal, to find inspiration in the rugged beauty of the Highlands. She had not come for ghost stories.

And yet, as she stepped back outside, the wind carrying the distant lapping of water against the shore, she could swear she heard something—

just a whisper, just a note — a melody
drifting from the loch.

Chapter 3: Echoes in The Mist

The morning dawned with a soft mist curling over the loch, swallowing the shoreline in wisps of silver. Isla sat on the small wooden porch of her cottage, wrapped in a thick woolen shawl she had picked up from the local shop. A cup of steaming tea warmed her hands as she gazed over the water, watching the way it barely rippled, eerily still beneath the rising sun.

Something about the loch unsettled her.

It wasn't just the way the villagers spoke of it in hushed tones or how they would glance toward the water and cross themselves. It wasn't even the odd, creeping sensation she had felt the night before when she stood at its edge. It was something deeper, something she couldn't quite name — like a whisper at the back of her mind, an echo of something long forgotten.

She shook herself. She was letting the atmosphere get to her. The entire reason she had come here was to escape her emotions, to lose herself in something other than grief.

With a deep breath, she rose from her seat and turned back into the cottage, determined to settle in properly. She had unpacked only the essentials last night, but now she took the time to place her paints and sketchbooks on the worn wooden desk near the window, where the light was best. A stack of well-worn books from her mother's collection sat on the small table beside the armchair, their familiar spines a comfort in an unfamiliar place.

She let her fingers trail over the titles, pausing on one in particular — an old volume of Celtic folklore, one she had loved since childhood. With a sigh, she pulled it from the stack and flipped through its pages absentmindedly, barely reading the words before snapping it shut. The past needed to stay in the past.

A sharp knock at the door startled her. Setting the book down, she walked over and pulled it open to reveal an older woman standing on the threshold. Her silver-streaked auburn hair was braided over one shoulder, her sharp eyes crinkling at the corners as she regarded Isla with a curious expression.

"You must be Miss Rowan," the woman said, her voice carrying the lilt of the Highlands. "I'm Morag. I run the grocer's down in the village. Brought you a few things to get you settled."

Isla stepped aside, motioning for her to enter. "That's very kind of you. Please, come in."

Morag bustled inside, setting a woven basket on the kitchen table. Fresh eggs, bread, butter, and a jar of golden honey peeked out from beneath a cloth. "I always like to make sure new folk have something decent to eat their first week," she said, glancing around the cottage. "It's been a while since anyone's stayed here."

Isla hesitated, then asked, "Why is that?"

Morag gave her a knowing look. "Same reason most folk don't linger too close to the loch at night."

A chill crept up Isla's spine. "The Loch's Lullaby?"

Morag's expression darkened slightly. "Aye. You've heard the stories, then?"

"Only whispers. A warning not to go near the water after dark." Isla forced a small laugh. "But surely that's just an old legend to scare outsiders?"

Morag didn't smile. "Legends start from truth, lass. And sometimes, they hold more truth than we'd like."

The air in the room grew heavier, the distant cry of a gull outside the only sound between them. Isla swallowed, resisting the urge to look toward the loch beyond the window.

"If you need anything," Morag continued, "you come down to the shop, aye? And Isla—" She met her gaze, serious now. "Don't go walking alone after sundown."

With that, she turned and let herself out, leaving Isla standing in the quiet cottage, the warnings of the village weighing heavier on her mind than before.

Chapter 4: The Melody

Isla had always believed that silence held a voice of its own. In the soft hush of the morning, as she stood at the edge of the loch, she could almost hear it whispering to her. The water stretched out before her, glassy and dark, reflecting the pale blue of the early sky. It was beautiful in a way that unsettled her, like a secret waiting to be unearthed.

She tightened the wool shawl around her shoulders, the chill of the Highlands creeping through the damp air. The village was quiet behind her, still waking, and she was grateful for the solitude. She had spent the past few days settling into the cottage, painting when she could, though inspiration was proving elusive. The grief of losing her mother still clung to her, heavy and suffocating, and her recent heartbreak had left her raw. She had come here to heal, but she hadn't anticipated the way the land itself seemed to pull at something deeper inside her.

The villagers had been kind but cautious, offering polite smiles and sidelong glances as if they knew something she did not. When she had asked about the loch's lullaby, the air in the pub had shifted, the older folk exchanging wary looks before one of them murmured a warning. "Best not to listen too closely," an elderly man had told her, his voice thick with unease. "Some songs aren't meant for the living."

Isla had brushed it off as mere superstition, but now, standing before the water, she wasn't so sure.

A gust of wind rippled the surface of the loch, and with it came something unexpected—a sound, faint but unmistakable. A melody, drifting over the water.

Her breath caught. It was hauntingly beautiful, a woman's voice carrying a tune both sorrowful and sweet. Isla turned, scanning the shoreline, but there was no one in sight. The village was still too far, and there was no sign of another soul near the loch.

A shiver ran down her spine.

She took a cautious step closer, her boots sinking slightly into the damp earth. The song wove through the air, its notes rising and falling like the ebb and flow of the tide. It beckoned her, stirring something deep within, something she couldn't name.

She knew she should turn back. Every instinct told her to walk away, to pretend she hadn't heard it. But Isla had never been one to ignore curiosity, even when it led her straight into the unknown.

So she stayed, listening, as the lullaby of the loch wrapped itself around her like a ghostly embrace.

Chapter 5: Beneath the Moonlit Sky

The night was still, save for the soft lapping of the loch against the shore. Isla had wandered farther than she intended, drawn by the quiet hush of the water, the silver light of the moon glistening upon its surface. The village whispers of the Loch's Lullaby played in the back of her mind, but she had dismissed them as old superstition.

She exhaled a breath, feeling the weight of her thoughts pressing heavily upon her. The loss of her mother, the heartbreak she had fled from — it all felt distant yet unbearably close. Her fingers traced the pendant at her throat, a small trinket she had carried with her since childhood, something to anchor her when the world felt too vast, too uncertain.

Then, a rustling behind her.

She turned sharply, her breath hitching. A tall figure emerged from the shadows of the trees lining the shore. For a fleeting moment, something within her stirred — something unexplainable, like a thread pulling taut in her chest.

"I didn't mean to startle ye," the man said, his voice rich and deep, with the unmistakable lilt of the Highlands. The moon illuminated his features — dark brown hair that curled slightly at the ends, green eyes that held a depth she couldn't look away from.

"It's alright," she found herself saying, though her heart was still racing. "I wasn't expecting anyone out here."

He gave a small chuckle, rubbing the back of his neck. "Aye, neither was I. But the loch — it has a way of callin' folk to it."

Isla studied him, the way his presence felt oddly familiar despite never having met him before. "Do you live here?"

"Aye," he nodded, stepping closer, though keeping a respectable distance. "Grew up here. Been away for a time, but… well, the Highlands have a way of pullin' ye back."

A silence stretched between them, not uncomfortable, but weighted with something unsaid. The night air carried the distant hoot of an owl, the whisper of the wind through the trees. Isla swallowed, gathering herself.

"I'm Isla Rowan," she offered, her voice softer now.

The man studied her for a moment before a small smile tugged at his lips. "Callum MaCrae." He extended a hand, and without hesitation, she placed hers in his. The moment their skin met, a shiver ran through her — not from the cold, but from something deeper. Recognition, perhaps, though she didn't know why.

Neither spoke of it. They simply stood there, hands clasped beneath the glow of the moon, the loch stretching before them like an unspoken promise.

Chapter 6: Shared Sorrow

The morning sun was gentle as it stretched over the loch, mist curling from the water's surface like lingering whispers. Isla sat on a moss-covered stone near the shore, sketchbook in hand, though her charcoal pencil hovered idly above the page. Her mind was elsewhere, still caught in the strange pull she had felt the night before—the song, the voice, the momentary flicker of something ancient in her chest.

Footsteps crunched over the frost-laced earth behind her. She turned just as Callum MaCrae emerged from the trees, his gaze shifting from her to the vast expanse of the loch. He carried a bundle of fishing nets slung over one shoulder, the weight of familiarity in his movements.

"Ye're up early," he remarked, his voice rich with the cadence of the Highlands.

Isla lifted a shoulder. "Couldn't sleep."

Callum nodded as though he understood all too well. He set his nets down and sat a few feet away, close enough that Isla could see the way his green eyes caught the light.

For a moment, they were quiet. The loch lapped softly against the shore, the world around them still waking.

Finally, Isla glanced at him, curiosity stirring.

"You said you're from here?" she asked.

"Aye." Callum exhaled, stretching his long legs out before him. "Born and raised. But I left for a time."

She sensed the weight in his words, something deeper than just a move from one place to another. "Why?"

His jaw tensed slightly, as if debating how much to say. "My grandfather passed."

Isla's fingers stilled on her sketchbook. "I'm sorry."

Callum shook his head. "He lived a long life. Taught me everything I know about the loch, the land, how to fish. But after he was gone… being here wasn't the same."

She watched the way his hands curled slightly, like they were remembering the feel of fishing line between his fingers. "So you left?"

"Aye." He glanced toward the water. "Took a job far away—something that kept me busy. Thought it'd help."

"And did it?" she asked softly.

His lips pressed together before he finally said, "For a while."

Silence stretched between them again, but it was not uncomfortable. There was an understanding in it, the kind that only those who had known loss could share. Isla looked down at her sketchbook and let out a breath.

"I lost my mother," she admitted, surprising even herself with the confession.

Callum's gaze snapped to her, the flicker of sorrow there immediate. "That's why ye came here?"

She nodded. "Needed to be somewhere quiet. Somewhere… away."

Callum's fingers traced over the worn wood of his nets. "Aye. I understand that."

The loch stretched before them, ancient and knowing, as if it had seen countless souls come and go, searching for something just as they were. The mist had begun to lift, revealing the water's true depth, the ripples that formed and disappeared as if they had never been.

Isla turned the page in her sketchbook, glancing at Callum. "Would you mind if I sketched you?"

His brows lifted slightly, but he let out a short chuckle. "Ye think I'd make a good subject?"

She smiled faintly. "You belong to this place. I think that makes you perfect for it."

Callum held her gaze for a moment before nodding. "Aye, then. If ye like."

As she lifted her pencil and let the first strokes form, something settled between them — something unspoken, yet undeniable. Two souls, both carrying loss, both drawn back to the same place. Neither of them knowing yet that the loch was not done with them. Not by a long shot.

Chapter 7: Invisible Pull

The morning mist still clung to the loch when Callum found himself walking the worn path toward the water's edge. He hadn't intended to come this way, but his feet seemed to have made the decision for him. The conversation with Isla the night before lingered in his mind, her presence stirring something he hadn't expected. It was a strange thing, how someone could feel both like a stranger and something familiar all at once.

As he stepped through the thinning trees, he saw her. She was perched on a flat rock near the shore, a wooden easel set up before her. A canvas stretched across it, barely touched yet, but already hinting at the beginning of something. The sight of her, utterly lost in her craft, held him still for a moment.

"You've got a skill for it," he said finally, his voice breaking the stillness between them.

Isla turned, a touch of surprise flickering across her face before she offered a small smile. "You think so? It's hardly started."

"Aye, but I can already tell," Callum said, stepping closer. His green eyes flicked to the soft strokes of color that had begun to shape the scene. "The way ye hold the brush, the way ye look at it—like ye already see it finished in yer mind."

She exhaled a quiet laugh. "Maybe I do. Or maybe I just get lost in it and hope for the best."

Callum lowered himself onto a nearby rock, the water lapping gently against the shore. "Could be the same thing. Either way, it's impressive."

She studied him for a moment, then returned her gaze to the loch. The air between them held an ease that neither fully understood, as if they had stepped into the middle of something that had already begun long before their first meeting.

Isla glanced at him from the corner of her eye. "You don't seem like the type to be interested in paintings."

He huffed a small laugh. "I'm no expert, that's true. But I can appreciate when someone's got a gift."

She dipped her brush into a swirl of paint, considering his words. "And what's your gift then, Callum MaCrae?"

His smile faded slightly, a shadow passing through his expression. "Used to be the sea," he admitted. "Still is, I suppose. Just… changed."

She tilted her head, curiosity sparking in her eyes. "Changed how?"

Callum hesitated, his fingers curling against his knee as he glanced out at the loch. The past had a way of pulling at him here, in this place that held so many memories. "That's a story for another time, I think."

Isla didn't press, sensing there was weight to his words. Instead, she dipped her brush again and turned back to the canvas. "Alright then," she said lightly. "Another time."

The gentle hush of the loch stretched between them, neither rushing to fill it. And somehow, that silence felt like the beginning of something neither of them could name just yet.

Chapter 8: Promise of Tomorrow

The days in the village moved with a quiet rhythm, time measured by the shifting tides of the loch and the slow unraveling of Isla's canvas. She had settled into a steady routine—mornings spent wandering the shoreline for inspiration, afternoons lost in brushstrokes, and evenings wrapped in the hush of the Highlands. Yet something had changed since meeting Callum MaCrae.

She thought of him more than she should. His voice, the way he seemed to belong to this place as much as the water and the hills, the way his presence lingered even after he was gone. It unsettled her, though she couldn't quite say why. Perhaps because, for the first time in a long while, she wasn't entirely alone with her thoughts.

A brisk wind swept through the glen as she made her way toward the village, the air crisp with the promise of rain. The sky was a stretch of muted grays, thick clouds rolling in from the west. As she passed the harbor, she spotted Callum at the docks, hauling crates from a small fishing boat with practiced ease. He moved like someone who had done this all his life, and perhaps he had.

She hesitated for only a moment before approaching.

"Hard at work, I see."

Callum turned, wiping his hands on a cloth, a half-smile curving his lips when he saw her. "Aye, the loch's no' just for looking at."

She huffed a quiet laugh. "I suppose not."

His gaze flicked to her hands, speckled with remnants of paint. "What are ye working on today?"

Isla glanced down, flexing her fingers as if seeing the evidence of her craft for the first time. "A landscape," she admitted. "Or at least, it will be. If it turns out the way I see it in my mind."

Callum tilted his head. "I imagine it will. Ye seem the sort who doesn't stop until things are just as they should be."

His words sent an unexpected warmth through her. "I suppose you're right about that."

A moment of silence stretched between them, the sound of the loch lapping gently against the dock. Then, Callum shifted, rubbing a hand over the back of his neck. "Would ye like to see a better view? There's a spot up by the cliffs—ye can see the whole loch from there. Might give ye inspiration."

Isla hesitated, surprised by the invitation, but there was something in his expression—genuine, open—that made her nod before she could second-guess herself. "I'd like that."

"Good," he said, his grin widening just slightly. "I'll take ye there tomorrow, then. Just after sunrise."

She didn't know why her heart beat faster at the thought, but she didn't fight it.

"Tomorrow, then," she agreed.

As she turned to leave, the wind picked up, carrying the scent of salt and something deeper — something older. It whispered over the water, curling around her like unseen hands.

And just beneath it, drifting from the loch's endless depths, she thought she heard a melody.

Soft. Haunting. Familiar

Chapter 9: The View

Isla woke before the sun had even begun to touch the horizon. A restless energy thrummed through her, an anticipation she couldn't shake. Today, Callum would take her to the cliffs — this secret place of his, a place that meant something to him. The thought sent a flutter through her chest, inexplicable yet undeniable.

She dressed quickly, pulling on layers to guard against the morning chill, and stepped outside. The village was still asleep, the world wrapped in the hush of dawn. Mist curled over the loch like ghostly fingers, shifting and swirling as if whispering secrets to those who would listen.

She made her way toward the docks, her breath clouding in the crisp air. The anticipation tightened in her stomach as she spotted Callum waiting for her, his hands tucked into his pockets, eyes scanning the horizon as though he, too, had been waiting for this moment longer than he could explain.

When he saw her, a slow, knowing smile tugged at his lips. "Ye're keen this morning."

She laughed, the sound breathless. "I could say the same about you."

He didn't deny it. Instead, he gestured for her to follow. "Come on, then. We've got a bit of a walk ahead of us."

They set off together, their steps crunching over frost-kissed grass as they made their way through the hills. The further they went, the wilder the landscape became, the cliffs rising in the distance like sentinels guarding something sacred. The wind picked up as they climbed, tugging at Isla's hair, stealing her breath, but she didn't care. Every step closer felt like stepping into something she wasn't sure she was ready for but couldn't turn away from.

When they reached the top, she let out a soft gasp. The world stretched endlessly before her—the water rolling into the horizon, the cliffs dropping into the abyss below, jagged and untamed. The sky, painted in early morning hues, seemed to wrap around them, endless and unbroken.

"It's breathtaking," she murmured.

Callum glanced at her, but he wasn't looking at the view. "Aye," he said quietly. "It is."

She turned to him, her pulse skittering. There was something in his gaze — something raw and unguarded. The wind whipped between them, but she felt nothing but the heat rolling off him, the way his presence wrapped around her like something tangible.

She didn't know who moved first. Maybe it was him. Maybe it was her. But suddenly, there was no space between them. His hands found her waist, grounding her, pulling her closer. Her fingers curled into the fabric of his coat, as if anchoring herself to him, to this moment.

When his lips met hers, it was as though the earth itself had paused. The kiss wasn't hesitant — it was deep, unyielding, filled with something that had been building between them from the moment they met. He tasted like salt and wind, like something ancient and unshakable. Isla melted into him, into the fire that surged through her, the undeniable pull between them.

And then—

A sound.

A melody carried on the wind, low and haunting.

The lullaby.

It slithered through the air, wrapping around them, cutting through the moment like a blade. Isla tensed, the hairs on her arms rising as the eerie tune curled around her senses, seeping into her bones.

Callum pulled back, his expression shifting, his jaw tightening.

For a moment, neither of them spoke.

Then, softly, Isla whispered, "Did you hear that?"

His gaze flickered toward the loch in the distance, dark and endless. "Aye," he said, his voice grave. "I did."

The moment between them had shifted, but something had been set in motion—something neither of them could stop now.

The moment shattered, but the fire it ignited did not extinguish. It still smoldered, lingering in the space between them.

Isla's heart pounded, torn between the rush of their stolen moment and the inexplicable unease that crept in with the song.

Callum exhaled slowly. "We should go."

She nodded, but as they walked back toward the village, she couldn't shake the feeling that the loch had been watching.

Chapter 10: The Lullaby

The morning light crept through the mist, weaving golden strands over the still surface of the loch. Isla stood at her easel near the cottage, her brush hovering above the canvas as her thoughts drifted to the day before. The memory of Callum's touch still burned on her skin, a warmth she hadn't felt in so long. And yet, just as quickly as it had ignited, the moment had been stolen away by that haunting melody. The lullaby had stirred something deep within her, something ancient and unrelenting.

She set her brush down with a sigh, rubbing her arms against the morning chill. She had barely slept, her dreams filled with shadowed figures and whispered voices. The loch, ever still and watchful, seemed different now — as though it had woken with her, waiting.

She turned to see Callum standing there, hands tucked into the pockets of his coat, his green eyes searching hers.

"Morning, lass," he greeted, his voice thick with something unreadable.

"Morning," she murmured, heart stuttering.

He stepped closer, glancing at her canvas. "Ye were up early."

She nodded. "I couldn't sleep."

Callum hesitated, as if debating whether to say something. "Aye, neither could I. Thought maybe a walk would clear my mind. I was wondering if ye'd join me."

Isla felt the air shift between them, heavy with something unspoken. A part of her wanted to retreat, to keep herself guarded. But another part, the part that had been drawn here without reason, told her she needed to go.

"Alright," she said finally.

They walked along the winding path leading away from the village, their steps slow, deliberate. Callum didn't speak right away, and neither did she. The silence between them wasn't uncomfortable — it pulsed with an anticipation neither of them acknowledged aloud.

The land rose before them. Isla inhaled sharply as they reached the edge of the far side of the loch, the wind tugging at her hair. Below, the loch stretched endlessly, its surface dark and beckoning.

"It's beautiful," she breathed.

Callum stood beside her, watching her rather than the view. "Aye, it is. My granddad used to bring me here as a lad. Said it was the one place where the world felt endless. Where ye could hear the loch speak if ye listened close enough."

Isla shivered, the memory of the lullaby stirring in her chest. "And have you? Heard it speak?"

Callum hesitated. "Aye," he admitted, voice quiet. "But only once."

She turned to him, searching his face. "When?"

"The night my granddad passed." His voice was raw, the weight of grief lingering even now. "I was out on the water. The air was still, the kind of silence that settles before a storm. And then, clear as day, I heard it—a song, drifting over the loch. Not just a sound, but a feeling. Like something old was mourning with me."

A chill ran down Isla's spine. "The lullaby."

Callum nodded slowly. "Aye."

The wind picked up around them, carrying a faint whisper over the cliffs. Isla swallowed hard, gripping the edge of her coat. She didn't know what to say, but Callum turned to her then, his gaze intense.

"Ye felt it too, didn't ye? Last night."

She hesitated, then nodded. "Yes."

His hand brushed against hers, a tentative touch that sent a spark through her veins. "Whatever it is, whatever's callin' us here… we'll figure it out. Together."

The word settled between them like an unspoken promise. Together. And for the first time since arriving in the Highlands, Isla felt she wasn't facing the unknown alone.

Chapter 11: Beneath the Surface

T he loch was glass-still, reflecting the night sky like a black mirror. Isla stood at its edge, the cold mist curling around her ankles, sending a shiver up her spine. She hadn't meant to wander this far after leaving Callum, but something had pulled her here, just as it had the night before. The melody—the one that had shattered their moment on the cliffs—was silent now, but she could feel it lingering, just beyond reach, waiting.

She knelt, dipping her fingers into the water. It was icy, unnaturally so for the season. The village whispers about the loch's curse flickered in her mind, but she brushed them aside. A lullaby couldn't harm her. A song, no matter how sorrowful, was not a ghost.

Yet, as she closed her eyes, she swore she heard something—soft, almost imperceptible, like a breath on the wind. A whisper.

Her heart leapt into her throat, and she pulled her hand back as if burned. The rational part of her told her it was only the wind shifting through the reeds, but deep down, something in her stirred—a feeling that she was not alone.

Callum hadn't been able to sleep. After Isla left, the air had felt different, charged with something unspoken. He found himself walking, his feet knowing the way before his mind caught up. The loch.

The moment he stepped through the trees and saw her standing at the water's edge, an uneasy feeling gripped him. The moonlight cast her in an ethereal glow, her red hair catching the silver light like fire beneath ice.

She turned as he approached, startled but not afraid. "Couldn't sleep?" she asked softly.

He shook his head, stepping closer. "And you?"

She hesitated, then exhaled, her breath visible in the cold air. "I keep hearing things. Maybe it's just my imagination, but… I don't know. I keep ending up here."

Callum's jaw tensed. The loch had always been steeped in superstition, but he'd never put much weight in old stories—until now. "It's late," he said, his voice low. "You shouldn't be out here alone."

A ghost of a smile touched her lips. "And yet, here you are."

His lips quirked, but there was no humor in his eyes. "Come on. I'll walk you back."

She hesitated, glancing back at the loch one last time. The surface remained still, betraying nothing. With a nod, she turned to him, falling into step beside him as they made their way back through the trees.

But just before they disappeared into the night, the wind shifted.

And the lullaby began again.

Chapter 12: Threads of the Past

The wind stirred as Callum and Isla walked side by side, the lullaby still lingering in the air, though softer now, as if the loch was whispering secrets only they could hear. Callum kept glancing at Isla from the corner of his eye. She walked with a quiet intensity, her arms wrapped around herself as though warding off more than just the cold.

He had the sudden urge to reach out, to anchor her in the present, but he resisted.

They reached the small cottage she had made her home, nestled just beyond the village's edge. The light of the hearth inside flickered through the window, casting golden hues against the dark. Isla turned to him, her face unreadable in the shadows.

"Thank you," she said softly. "For walking me back."

Callum nodded, but neither of them moved. The air between them felt heavy with something unsaid. Finally, he exhaled, glancing back toward the loch. "You should be careful near the water," he murmured. "The stories—"

"Do you believe them?" she interrupted, tilting her head.

He hesitated. Before, he might have dismissed them outright. But something about the past few days—

about Isla, about the way the loch seemed to call her—had him questioning everything. "I don't know anymore," he admitted.

A small smile ghosted across her lips. "Neither do I."

She turned to go, but before she disappeared inside, she hesitated at the threshold. "Would you—" She paused, almost as if reconsidering. "Would you come by tomorrow?."

Callum studied her for a moment before nodding. "Aye. I will."

Isla lingered for a second longer, then slipped inside, the door closing softly behind her.

That night, neither of them slept well.

Isla sat in front of her easel, staring at the canvas she had started earlier that day. It was nothing but rough strokes, the beginnings of a landscape, but the image in her mind was clear—

the loch, the cliffs, the mist rolling over the water like an ethereal veil. And there, just beneath the surface, something waiting.

She shivered and set her brush down.

Memories of the past few days mingled with dreams she couldn't quite remember, and for the first time in a long time, she felt as though she was standing at the edge of something she couldn't explain.

Callum sat on the small wooden porch of his grandfather's cottage, staring out at the water. The night was still, save for the occasional rustling of the trees. He thought of Isla, of the way she seemed drawn to this place, just as he had been. Just as he always had been, even when he tried to leave it behind.

He ran a hand over his face. It wasn't just the loch. It was her. There was something familiar about the way she carried herself, about the way she listened to the silence as if it might speak to her. And for the first time since returning, he wondered if he wasn't the only one searching for something lost.

With a sigh, he stood and turned toward the door. He needed sleep.

But as he stepped inside, the wind picked up, and across the loch, the lullaby began again.

Chapter 13: The Echo of Her Name

The morning mist clung to the hills, thick and low, as Isla made her way down to the village. The weight of the previous night sat heavy on her chest—the voice on the wind, the song, the way Callum had looked at her with an unspoken understanding. She hadn't been able to shake the feeling that something was shifting, like she was teetering on the edge of uncovering something buried deep in the past.

She needed a distraction. Something tangible. Something real. So she found herself at the village market, weaving between stalls of fresh bread, smoked fish, and handcrafted goods. The scents of peat smoke and salt mingled in the air, grounding her, reminding her she was still in the present, even as the past whispered just beneath the surface.

"Ye're up early, lass."

Isla turned to find an older woman watching her with sharp eyes, a basket of herbs resting on her hip. Mrs. MacTavish, the village healer. Isla had only spoken to her once or twice, but she had the feeling the woman knew far more than she let on.

Isla said, managing a small smile. "Thought I'd explore a bit."

Mrs. MacTavish hummed, her gaze lingering on Isla as if weighing something. "Ye dream last night?"

The question sent a chill through Isla's spine. "Why would you ask that?"

The woman shrugged, plucking a sprig of lavender from her basket and rolling it between her fingers. "The loch has a way of speaking to those who listen. And those who don't."

Isla swallowed hard. She wasn't ready to admit anything—to this woman, to herself. Instead, she cleared her throat. "Do ye know much about the lullaby?"

Mrs. MacTavish's lips pressed into a thin line. "More than most would care to know."

"Then tell me," Isla pressed. "Please."

The woman sighed, glancing around before leaning in slightly. "It's an old song, older than any of us.

Some say it was born of sorrow, others say it was a warning. But one thing is certain — those who hear it are part of its story, whether they want to be or not."

A shiver ran through Isla. Before she could ask more, a familiar voice broke through the hum of the market.

"There ye are."

She turned to find Callum striding toward her, his presence as steady and grounding as the earth beneath her feet. His hair was tousled, as if he'd been against the wind, his expression unreadable but intent.

"Callum," she said, relief slipping into her voice before she could stop it.

He gave Mrs. MacTavish a respectful nod before his eyes settled on Isla. "I was hoping to find ye here. Fancy a walk?"

Mrs. MacTavish watched them for a beat before handing Isla the sprig of lavender. "For clarity," she murmured before turning away.

Isla swallowed hard, tucking the herb into her pocket as she met Callum's gaze. "I'd like that."

As they walked through the village and toward the hills, the lullaby whispered at the edges of her mind, like a secret waiting to be unraveled.

Chapter 14: Myths Start From Truth

As Isla and Callum walked through the village, the noise of the market faded behind them, replaced by the rustling of leaves and the distant lap of water against the loch's shore. The scent of lavender still lingered in Isla's hands, mixing with the crisp air as she tucked the sprig deeper into her pocket.

They walked in silence for a while, their steps naturally falling into rhythm. Isla stole a glance at Callum, noting the quiet intensity in his features. There was something grounding about him, something that made her feel less untethered, even as her mind churned with unanswered questions.

"Ye looked deep in thought back there," Callum finally said, his voice steady, though his gaze remained fixed on the path ahead.

She exhaled, tracing her fingers over the rough stitching of her cloak. "Aye. Mrs. MacTavish… she spoke of the lullaby. Of the loch."

His steps faltered for the briefest moment before continuing. "And what did she say?"

"That those who hear it are part of its story. Whether they want to be or not."

Callum was quiet, his jaw tightening just enough for Isla to notice. The reaction sent a ripple of unease through her. "Ye've heard it again, haven't ye?"

She hesitated before nodding. "Last night. At the water's edge. It was different this time… closer. It felt—"

"Like it was meant for ye." Callum's voice was low, as if he was speaking a truth neither of them wanted to admit aloud.

Isla stopped walking, forcing him to turn toward her. "What do ye know, Callum? Truly?" Her voice was soft but insistent, the wind carrying her words between them.

For a moment, he seemed to struggle, torn between caution and confession. His fingers curled into fists at his sides, then relaxed as he exhaled. "More than I wish I did."

A shiver danced up Isla's spine. "Tell me."

Callum looked past her, his gaze settling on the dark silhouette of the cliffs in the distance. "Not here. Come with me."

She didn't hesitate. Without another word, he took her hand—warm, steady, reassuring—and led her away from the well-worn path. The land sloped gently at first, then steepened as they climbed, weaving through heather and stone. The loch stretched wide below them, the village now no more than a scatter of rooftops nestled in the valley.

Finally, they reached a ridge where the wind howled through the crags. Callum let go of her hand and turned to face her, the weight of something unspoken in his eyes.

"Isla," he said, voice roughened by the wind. "There are things about this place, about the past, that are not just stories. And if ye keep listening to that song… ye may find yerself caught in something ye cannae walk away from."

Isla's heart pounded. "Then help me understand it. Help me understand why I can't ignore it."

Callum studied her for a long moment, as if weighing something precious in his hands. Then, with a breath that seemed to carry a lifetime of ghosts, he nodded.

"I will. But what I tell ye… ye must promise not to turn away."

The lullaby drifted faintly on the wind, a whisper threading between them.

Isla met his gaze, her resolve unshaken. "I promise."

Chapter 15: The Missing Ruins

The wind howled through the ridge, whipping Isla's hair against her face as she stood beside Callum. The weight of his words pressed against her chest, heavier than the air thick with the scent of heather and distant rain.

She had promised not to turn away. And she wouldn't.

Callum's eyes searched hers for a long moment, then he exhaled, his gaze drifting past her toward the loch. "The stories of this place… they're not just old tales meant to frighten children. There's truth woven into them, buried beneath the years."

Isla shivered, though not entirely from the cold. "Truth?"

He gave a slow nod. "A long time ago, before the village was what it is now, there was another—one that stood closer to the loch's edge. It's gone now, lost to time, but its people… their voices are not."

The lullaby flickered in the back of Isla's mind, a haunting thread winding its way through her memories. She swallowed hard. "What happened to them?"

Callum hesitated, his fingers curling into the fabric of his coat as if bracing himself. "No one knows for certain. One day, they were there. The next… nothing remained but silence. No ruins, no graves—just the loch and the song…and one cottage."

A chill ran down Isla's spine. "And ye think the lullaby is tied to them?"

He let out a low breath. "I know it is."

A crack of thunder rumbled in the distance, though the sky remained clear. Isla's pulse quickened. "Callum… have ye heard it too?"

His jaw tensed, and for a moment, she thought he wouldn't answer. But then he gave a slow, measured nod. "Aye. Since I was a boy."

The confession stole the breath from her lungs. She had been so certain she was alone in this—that the song had chosen her for some unknown reason. But if Callum had heard it too…

"Why?" she asked, her voice barely above a whisper. "Why us?"

"I don't know," he admitted, running a hand through his dark hair. "But I do know this—those who hear it are never the same."

A heavy silence settled between them, broken only by the distant call of a bird and the whisper of the wind through the crags. Isla clenched her hands at her sides. "Then we have to find out what it wants. We have to understand it."

Callum's expression darkened. "That's what I'm afraid of."

Before Isla could press further, the wind shifted, carrying a sound so soft, so sorrowful, it made her breath catch.

The lullaby.

Not distant this time. Not faint.

It was here.

And it was calling her name.

Chapter 16: Sacred Cottage

Callum led Isla through the tangled embrace of the woods, the canopy above weaving shadows that danced with the shifting light. He moved with purpose, though Isla sensed a weight in each step, as if he were crossing an invisible threshold.

"This place…" he began, voice quieter than usual. "I found it when I was a boy. I never told anyone."

She glanced at him, curiosity piqued. "Why?"

He hesitated, pushing past a thick branch, then stepped aside so she could follow. "Because it never felt like it belonged to the world we know." He exhaled slowly, his fingers brushing against the moss-covered stones they passed. "The first time I saw it, I'd wandered too far from home. A storm had rolled in, and I was trying to find shelter. That's when I found the house."

A shiver ran down Isla's spine as the wind whispered through the trees. "Ye mean this house?"

He nodded. "Aye. But it felt… untouched by time. Sacred, almost. Even as a lad, I knew better than to disturb what wasn't mine to claim. So I never spoke of it. Not until now."

As they stepped into a clearing, Isla's breath caught. Nestled between the trees, the house stood in solemn silence. Time had worn its edges, ivy creeping up its stone walls, but it held an undeniable grace—like a secret frozen in time. The air around it felt different, heavier, as if the past still lingered within its walls, waiting.

Isla reached out, trailing her fingers over the wooden door. The grain was rough beneath her touch, the iron handle cool. "She lived here, didn't she?"

Callum stepped closer, his gaze dark with something unspoken. "Aye."

The weight of the moment settled between them, thick as the mist curling at their feet. Isla swallowed, her heartbeat a steady drum against her ribs. "Tell me."

Callum exhaled, his eyes tracing the edges of the house as if seeing the echoes of a life long past. "She wasn't a witch, Isla." His voice was gentle, firm. "She was a woman who loved. A woman who lost."

He stepped toward the door and pushed it open. It groaned on its hinges, revealing the dim interior. Dust motes swirled in the slanted beams of light breaking through the cracks in the shutters. A hearth stood cold and empty, but remnants of a life remained—faded tapestries, a wooden chair tucked beneath an old table, a shelf lined with brittle, long-forgotten books.

"She was meant to marry another," Callum continued, his voice steady despite the sorrow woven through it. "A cruel man. Cold, unyielding. But her heart already belonged to another." He stepped deeper inside, his fingers grazing the back of a chair. "They would meet here. This was their escape."

Isla's throat tightened. "Until he found out."

Callum nodded. "And when he did… he ended it. Took the life of the man she loved and left her with nothing but grief." His gaze lifted to Isla's, unreadable. "So she sang."

The silence between them was thick with understanding. The lullaby — the sorrow woven into its melody — wasn't just a song. It was a lament, a wound that never closed.

"She walked into the loch," Isla whispered, the realization settling deep in her chest. "And the song never stopped."

"No." Callum's voice was barely more than breath. "It waits."

A chill swept through Isla, though the air was still. She turned, her eyes scanning the room, as if expecting to see her shadow stretch alongside another's. "For what?"

Callum's jaw tightened. "That's what we need to find out."

And as if in answer, the distant echo of the lullaby threaded through the trees, carried by the wind like a secret begging to be heard.

Chapter 17: Love Lost

The air inside the cottage was thick with silence, as though the walls held their breath, waiting. Isla let her fingers skim the edge of an old wooden table, dust rising in tiny, swirling ghosts. Everything in the space felt untouched yet somehow alive, steeped in memories neither of them could see.

Callum stood just inside the doorway, his eyes sweeping the room with quiet reverence. "I didnae come here often," he admitted. "Only a handful of times after I first found it. Something about it always felt... sacred. As if it belonged to someone else, even after all this time."

Isla turned, watching him as he spoke. "Yet you brought me here."

His gaze met hers, steady. "Aye. Because I think it was meant for ye."

The weight of his words settled deep in her chest. She turned away, drawing in a slow breath as she moved to the stone hearth. A cold fireplace, the embers long gone. She traced her fingers along the carved mantle, her touch ghosting over the initials etched into the wood. Time had worn them down, but she could still make out two letters: 'M' and 'A'.

"Their names," she whispered.

Callum stepped closer, his voice low. "Aye. .Maeve and Angus"

The names settled on her tongue like an old song. "Ye knew them?"

"Only what I could piece together," he admitted. "The old stories, the whispers in the village. But it's different when ye stand here, when ye see the mark they left behind."

Isla swallowed hard. She could feel it too—the presence of something just out of reach, lingering in the very air. Her fingers curled against the mantle. "She loved him enough to risk everything."

Callum nodded. "And he loved her enough to die for it."

A chill curled down Isla's spine. "The man she was meant to wed—he killed Angus, didn't he?"

Callum's jaw tensed. "Aye. Struck him down in cold blood when he found them together. Some say Maeve cursed the loch with her sorrow, that the lullaby she sang was her grief made eternal. Others say it was no curse at all, only a love that refused to fade."

Isla closed her eyes for a moment, listening. The air in the cottage was heavy, but not with fear. It was longing, aching, waiting.

She turned back to Callum. "I hear it still, Callum. The song. Even now."

His eyes darkened. "Then the story's not finished yet."

A gust of wind rattled the wooden shutters, and outside, the loch stretched wide and endless. A question hung between them, unspoken yet undeniable.

If the lullaby was waiting, then what—or who—was it waiting for?

Chapter 18: The Past is Calling

By the time Isla and Callum emerged from the old, hidden cottage, the sky had darkened with the weight of an impending storm. The first drops of rain were light, cool against Isla's flushed skin, but within moments, the heavens fully opened, drenching them in a relentless downpour.

They hurried down the narrow, winding path toward the village, the rain turning the earth beneath their feet slick and treacherous. Isla's cloak clung to her, heavy with water, and her boots squelched with each step. Callum stayed close, his fingers brushing her arm every so often, steadying her when she slipped on the uneven ground.

By the time they reached the door of her cottage, they were both soaked through. Isla pushed open the door, stepping inside and shivering as the warmth of the small space wrapped around her. She turned back to Callum, hesitating only for a moment before saying, "You should come in. At least until the rain passes."

Callum hesitated, glancing back at the downpour before nodding. "Aye. Thank ye."

She stepped aside to let him in, closing the door behind them. The storm raged on outside, rain hammering against the roof, the wind rattling the shutters. Inside, it was quiet but for the sound of their breathing and the faint crackle of the hearth's embers, still holding the last warmth from earlier in the day.

Isla peeled off her soaked cloak, draping it over a chair. Callum did the same, running a hand through his damp hair, sending droplets scattering onto the wooden floor. Isla turned to the small chest by the hearth, rummaging through it until she found a dry tunic and a woolen blanket.

"Ye should change," she said, holding the tunic out to him. "Yer soaked through."

His lips quirked slightly, though his eyes held a flicker of something unreadable. "And ye?"

She hesitated before nodding toward the modest partition that separated her sleeping space from the main room. "I'll change as well."

They turned away from each other, the small space making the moment feel even more intimate. Isla untied the laces of her dress with careful fingers, peeling the wet fabric away from her skin. The woolen shift she pulled on was warm, dry, clinging softly to her curves. She exhaled, adjusting the sleeves before turning — only to catch Callum's reflection in the small mirror hanging near the hearth.

He had his back to her, pulling the dry tunic over his head, muscles shifting beneath his skin. For a brief moment, she let herself look, let herself take in the way the firelight cast shadows over the hard planes of his body. And then, as if sensing her gaze, Callum turned.

Their eyes met, the air between them shifting, charged. Neither of them spoke. Neither of them looked away.

Isla's breath caught, her fingers tightening around the edge of the blanket she hadn't realized she was still holding. Callum's expression was unreadable, but there was something in his gaze—something raw, something that sent a shiver down her spine that had nothing to do with the cold.

The fire crackled, breaking the spell. Isla swallowed, turning away first. "I'll fix us some tea."

Callum cleared his throat, running a hand over the back of his neck. "Aye. That sounds good."

She moved to the hearth, focusing on the familiar rhythm of preparing tea—pouring water into the kettle, setting it over the flames. The tension in the air still lingered, but the simple task gave her something to hold onto. Callum settled onto the bench near the fire, stretching his long legs out in front of him.

A few moments later, Isla set two steaming cups on the table. She sat across from him, pulling the blanket around her shoulders. They drank in silence at first, the warmth of the tea seeping into their bones. Then, slowly, the conversation returned — not to the tension that had just filled the room, but to what they had discovered in the hidden cottage.

"The story feels closer now," Isla murmured, tracing the rim of her cup. "Like it's not just something from the past. Like it's still happening."

Callum nodded, his gaze steady. "Maybe it is. Maybe it never truly ended."

She looked up at him, and for a moment, she wasn't sure if they were still speaking about Maeve and Angus — or something else entirely.

Chapter 19: Fire Crackles

The rain had slowed to a steady drizzle by the time Isla and Callum finished their tea, but neither of them made any move to acknowledge it. The air inside the cottage had grown thick with something unspoken, something neither of them seemed willing to break.

Callum leaned back in his chair, rolling his now-empty cup between his palms. His damp shirt clung to his skin, the firelight casting shadows across the fabric. Isla tried not to stare, tried to focus on the gentle crackle of the fire instead, but her thoughts betrayed her. The memory of him standing there, shirtless, his back turned as they changed, lingered far too vividly in her mind.

She swallowed, suddenly feeling too warm despite the chill that still clung to the air. "It's still raining," she murmured, more to fill the silence than anything else.

Callum's gaze lifted to hers, unreadable. "Aye."

The single word sent a shiver down her spine. There was something about the way he looked at her now, something different than before. It wasn't just curiosity or concern—it was awareness. A charged stillness settled between them, and Isla found herself gripping her cup a little tighter.

"Ye don't have to stay," she said, though the words felt hollow. "If ye need to be going—"

"I dinnae mind the rain," he interrupted, his voice quiet but firm. He set his cup down, leaning forward slightly. "Unless ye want me to go?"

Isla's breath caught. Did she?

The rational part of her knew that whatever was happening between them was dangerous. She was here to uncover a mystery, to understand why the lullaby had called to her across time and distance. But Callum... Callum had become part of that story in ways she hadn't expected. And now, sitting across from him, her heart pounding beneath the weight of his gaze, she wasn't sure where the lines blurred between history and the present.

"No," she admitted softly. "I don't want you to go."

Something flickered in Callum's expression, something unreadable yet intense. He pushed back his chair and stood, moving toward the fire. The flickering glow illuminated the sharp angles of his face, the droplets of rain still clinging to his hair.

"This place," he murmured, as though speaking more to himself than to her, "it changes things."

Isla rose slowly, drawn to him by something she couldn't name. "What do you mean?"

He turned to face her, his gaze searching hers. "The past and the present—here, they feel like the same thing. Like whatever happened all those years ago is still happening, just waiting to be rewritten."

She shivered, not from the cold, but from the truth in his words. "And what do you think needs to be rewritten?"

Callum's jaw tensed slightly. He took a step toward her, closing the space between them. "I think some stories are never meant to end."

The words sent a jolt through her, a deep, aching pull that she felt down to her bones. Her pulse quickened as he reached up, tucking a damp strand of hair behind her ear. His fingers brushed against her skin, warm despite the lingering chill, and she swore the entire world narrowed to that single point of contact.

"Callum—" she started, but she didn't know what she meant to say.

He exhaled, his breath mingling with hers. "Tell me to stop, Isla. If ye want me to."

She knew she should. That she should step back, put distance between them before they crossed a line neither of them could return from. But she didn't move. Didn't speak.

Because she didn't want him to stop.

The fire crackled, the rain tapped softly against the windows, and in that quiet, suspended moment, Isla knew she was standing on the edge of something she couldn't turn away from.

And she wasn't sure she wanted to.

Chapter 20:

Whispering Rain

The rain had slowed to a whisper against the windows, but inside the cottage, the storm had only just begun. Isla stood frozen in place, her heart pounding in rhythm with the raindrops. Callum was so close now, the warmth of his body cutting through the chill of their damp clothes, the firelight flickering against the sharp planes of his face.

She could still feel the weight of his touch where his fingers had brushed her cheek, and the ghost of it sent a shiver down her spine. Her breath came unsteady as she searched his eyes, looking for some reason to step away, some reason to break whatever spell had settled over them. But she found none.

Callum exhaled, his gaze locked onto hers with an intensity that sent heat curling low in her stomach. He had asked her to tell him to stop. He had given her that choice. But she hadn't taken it.

Instead, she reached for him.

Her fingers found the damp fabric of his shirt, hesitating for only a moment before curling into it. The movement was small, tentative, but it was enough. Callum's breath hitched, and then, in the space of a heartbeat, his lips were on hers.

The kiss was slow at first, deliberate, as though they were both testing the weight of it, the feel of it. But then Callum's hands came to rest at her waist, his grip firm, grounding, and something inside Isla unraveled. She pressed closer, deepening the kiss, losing herself in the warmth of him, in the way he tasted like rain and fire and something distinctly him.

A sharp crack from the fireplace startled them apart, their breaths ragged. Callum's forehead rested against hers, his hands still holding her as though he wasn't quite ready to let go.

"Isla," he murmured, his voice rough with something she didn't dare name.

She swallowed hard, her hands still fisted in his shirt. "We should—"

He pulled back slightly, his gaze searching hers. "Should what?"

She opened her mouth, but no words came. What should they do? Step away? Pretend this hadn't happened? The very thought of it sent a sharp pang through her chest.

Callum's thumb brushed against her hip, a slow, grounding touch. "Tell me what ye want."

Isla's throat went dry. What did she want? It should have been simple, but nothing about this was simple. And yet, looking at him now, feeling the solid weight of him against her, the answer was suddenly the easiest thing in the world.

"You," she whispered.

Something shifted in Callum's expression, a flicker of something raw and unguarded. He lifted his hand to cup her face, his thumb tracing a gentle line along her cheek. "Aye, lass," he murmured, his voice thick. "I want ye too."

The words sent a shiver through her, and then he was kissing her again, deeper this time, with a hunger that sent the world tilting beneath her feet. She melted into him, her fingers threading into his damp hair, pulling him closer as if that could somehow make up for all the moments they had resisted this.

Somewhere in the back of her mind, she knew this changed everything. Knew that there would be no going back from this moment, no pretending they could ignore whatever was pulling them together. But right now, with Callum's arms around her, with the fire crackling beside them and the rain a distant murmur against the window, she didn't care.

For once, she let herself fall.

Chapter 21: Seductive Surrender

The fire crackled softly, casting flickering shadows along the stone walls of the cottage. The rain had all but stopped, leaving only the occasional drip from the eaves, but inside, the storm between them had only just begun. Isla felt the weight of Callum's gaze, heavy with something raw, something unspoken that had been simmering beneath the surface for far too long.

Her breath came uneven, her fingers still tangled in the damp fabric of his shirt. He hadn't moved away. Neither had she. There was no space between them now, only the warmth of his body and the pounding of her own heart.

Callum lifted a hand, tracing the line of her jaw with a touch so gentle it sent shivers through her. His thumb brushed her lower lip, a breath of a touch, but it was enough to make her pulse stutter. He watched her, waiting, his restraint a taut wire between them.

"Say the word, Isla," he murmured, his voice rough, strained. "And I'll stop."

She should have hesitated, should have let her mind catch up to the fire raging through her veins. But she didn't. She couldn't. Because the truth was, she didn't want him to stop.

Instead of answering, she rose onto her toes, closing the remaining space between them, her lips brushing his in a silent plea. That was all it took.

Callum groaned, his control snapping like a bowstring. His hands slid to her waist, strong and sure as he pulled her flush against him, deepening the kiss. There was no hesitation now, no caution. Only need. His mouth moved over hers with a hunger that sent heat pooling low in her belly, a dizzying blend of urgency and something far more dangerous—something that felt like surrender.

She clung to him as if he were the only thing anchoring her to this moment, her hands sliding beneath the damp fabric of his shirt, seeking the heat of his skin. He hissed against her lips as her fingers traced the hard planes of his back, his muscles tensing beneath her touch. Then, in one swift motion, he pulled the shirt over his head and tossed it aside, leaving nothing between them but the whisper of her own breath.

Isla swallowed hard, her fingers hesitating at the sight of him — broad and strong, his skin marred with the faintest traces of scars that told stories she hadn't yet heard. He was beautiful in a way that made her chest ache, in a way that made her want to know every part of him, not just with her hands but with her heart.

"Ye keep looking at me like that, lass," Callum rasped, his voice thick with restraint, "and I won't be able to keep myself from taking ye right here."

A slow, deliberate heat unfurled in her stomach at his words. Her lips parted, but no sound came. She felt powerless against the pull of him, lost in the way his eyes burned into hers, in the way his chest rose and fell with every ragged breath.

Then he was on her again, his lips trailing fire along her throat, over the sensitive skin at the hollow of her collarbone. Her head tipped back, a soft gasp escaping as he pressed her against the warmth of the stone hearth, his hands roaming, mapping every curve as if he were committing her to memory.

Isla's fingers found his hair, tugging just enough to pull his gaze back to hers. Her breath shuddered. "I don't want you to hold back."

Something dark and wild flashed in his expression. He cupped her face, his thumb sweeping over her cheek with a tenderness that contradicted the intensity in his eyes. "Are ye sure?"

She nodded, her heart hammering. "I've never been more sure of anything."

Callum exhaled sharply, as if the weight of her words had undone him. Then he kissed her again — deep, claiming, as if he was making a promise neither of them could take back. And Isla, for once, let herself believe in it, let herself drown in the fire between them, knowing that after this moment, there would be no going back.

And not wanting to.

Chapter 22: Fate

The embers in the hearth glowed low, casting a golden sheen over the room, their heat rivaled only by the fire smoldering between them. The cottage had fallen into a hush, the rain outside no longer drumming against the windows, but inside, the storm raged on, quiet and unrelenting.

Isla lay against the solid warmth of Callum, her breath still unsteady, her skin alight with the remnants of his touch. She had never felt anything like this—this aching closeness, this bone-deep certainty that she was exactly where she was meant to be. The weight of his arm draped over her, anchoring her, his fingertips tracing idle patterns along her spine.

"Ye're quiet," Callum murmured, his voice rough with the edges of sleep, but beneath it, there was something else—something careful, something cautious.

Isla turned her head, meeting his gaze in the dim light. His eyes, dark and unreadable, searched hers as if bracing for something he didn't want to hear.

"I was just thinking," she admitted, her fingers idly tracing the ridges of his knuckles. "That maybe fate isn't as cruel as I thought."

A flicker of something softened the hard line of his jaw, but he said nothing, only watched her as if memorizing the way she looked in this moment. The firelight painted his features in gold and shadow, his tousled hair falling over his forehead, his lips swollen from the force of their kisses.

Callum exhaled slowly, his hand sliding up her back, his fingers tangling in her hair. "Isla," he murmured, and something in the way he said her name sent a shiver through her.

She knew what he wasn't saying. That this changed everything. That there was no turning back. And she knew, without a doubt, that she didn't want to.

She leaned in, pressing her lips to his, slow and lingering. He responded instantly, his grip tightening, pulling her flush against him. There was no urgency now, no desperate need — only something deeper, something that tethered them together beyond desire alone.

When they parted, Callum rested his forehead against hers. "I can't promise ye an easy road, lass," he said, his voice hushed but firm. "But I can promise ye this—I will always fight for ye. If ye'll let me."

A lump formed in Isla's throat. She had spent so long running—from her past, from her feelings, from the fear of wanting too much and losing it all. But Callum wasn't something she could run from. He was something she wanted to run toward.

So she gave him the only answer that mattered.

"I don't want easy," she whispered. "I want you."

Callum's breath hitched, and for a moment, he simply looked at her as if trying to commit every part of her to memory. Then, with a quiet groan, he pulled her beneath him, kissing her slow and deep, as if sealing a promise between them.

Outside, the storm had passed. But inside, something new had begun.

Chapter 23: Sense of Doom

The morning light crept through the cracks in the shutters, golden rays slicing through the lingering darkness. The fire had long since burned to embers, casting only the faintest warmth against the cool air of the cottage. Isla stirred first, blinking slowly as her senses returned to her. The weight of the night settled over her, not as a burden, but as something irrevocable, something precious.

Callum's arm was draped over her waist, his warmth anchoring her even as the rest of the world felt unsteady. She turned her head slightly, her gaze tracing the strong lines of his face as he slept—relaxed in a way she had never seen before. The usual intensity that burned behind his eyes was gone, replaced by something softer, something vulnerable. It made her heart ache in ways she hadn't expected.

She reached out, fingers brushing over the curve of his shoulder, tracing the faint scars that marked his skin. Battle scars, she realized. Stories she hadn't yet heard. The thought sent a pang through her—she wanted to know everything, every part of him, the past that shaped him, the burdens he carried.

As if sensing her touch, Callum shifted, a low hum escaping his throat. His arm tightened around her, pulling her closer before his eyes even opened. When they did, they were heavy with sleep but still piercing, still consuming in the way only he could manage. A slow, lazy smile tugged at his lips.

"Morning, lass." His voice was thick with sleep, rough and intimate in the quiet of the room.

A flush crept up her neck, but she didn't look away. Instead, she offered a small smile of her own. "Morning."

His fingers traced idle patterns along her spine, sending shivers in their wake. "How are ye feeling?"

She exhaled a soft laugh, tilting her head as if considering. "Sore," she admitted, "but… happy."

His grin widened, mischief flickering in his gaze. "Aye, I'd be offended if ye weren't."

She swatted his arm playfully, but he caught her wrist, tugging her hand to his lips. The kiss was soft, reverent, and the shift in his expression made her breath catch.

"Isla," he murmured, his thumb brushing against her palm. "Last night…"

Her heart stuttered. She knew what he was asking, what he was trying to say. Last night had changed everything, but neither of them had dared voice what that truly meant.

She swallowed, her fingers tightening around his. "I don't regret it."

Something eased in his expression, though the intensity remained. He cupped her face then, tilting it so she had no choice but to meet his gaze. "Nor do I."

The words settled between them, solid and unshakable. She could see it in his eyes—the same terrifying, exhilarating certainty that mirrored her own.

A knock at the door shattered the moment.

They both froze, the spell between them breaking as reality came crashing in. Callum's expression darkened instantly, all traces of warmth vanishing. He moved swiftly, rolling from the bed and reaching for his discarded shirt. Isla sat up, clutching the blanket to her chest as she tried to steady her racing heart.

Another knock—firmer this time. Whoever it was, they weren't leaving.

Callum shot her a quick glance, his expression unreadable before he strode toward the door. He cracked it open just enough to see who stood on the other side. Isla couldn't hear the exchange, but she saw the way Callum's shoulders tensed, the way his jaw locked.

A heartbeat later, he turned back to her, his expression grim.

"We need to go," he said, his voice laced with urgency. "Now."

Isla's stomach twisted. Whatever peace they had found in the quiet of the morning had just been shattered.

And she had the sinking feeling that everything was about to change.

Chapter 24: Haunted Waters

The air inside the cottage had shifted—something unseen but tangible, like the whisper of a storm on the horizon. Isla felt it in the way Callum tensed beside her, in the way the morning light no longer seemed quite as warm. The knock at the door had not been urgent, nor had it been a warning. But it had been unexpected.

Callum turned back to her, his expression unreadable. "Stay here," he murmured before slipping out into the cool morning air. Isla sat up, clutching the blanket to her chest, her heart still pounding from the intimacy they had shared mere moments ago.

She strained to listen, catching only muffled voices beyond the door. When Callum returned, his jaw was tight, his gaze shadowed with something she couldn't place.

"Who was it?" she asked softly.

"A messenger from the village," he replied, raking a hand through his hair. "They need me to come at once. There's been... an incident."

A chill ran through her. "What kind of incident?"

Callum hesitated, his brows drawing together. "A fisherman swears he saw a woman on the shore last night—singing. Said she vanished into the mist before he could call out to her. And then... this morning, his boat was found adrift, oars missing. No sign of him anywhere."

Isla's breath caught. "The Loch's Lullaby."

He nodded. "Aye. They think it's happening again."

A shiver danced down Isla's spine. She had learned the stories since coming here, all the warnings to stay away from the loch—the woman who had sung her grief to the loch and disappeared within, her sorrow so deep it had become legend. Some claimed her spirit lingered, but she had never heard the part of the story where her song called men to their doom, dragging them into the depths. She had been feeling something eerie about the loch as of late, but dismissed it as her own deep feelings unrvalleing from her own loss and new found desire.

Until now.

She rose from the bed, reaching for her discarded gown. "I'm coming with you."

Callum's expression hardened. "Isla—"

"No." She met his gaze, unwavering. "I need to see this for myself."

He studied her for a long moment, then exhaled sharply. "Fine. But stay close to me."

Together, they set off toward the village, the weight of the legend pressing upon them both. Isla wasn't sure what they would find when they arrived, but one thing was certain.

The past was no longer content to remain a story. And whatever truth lay beneath the legend of the Loch's Lullaby was waiting to be uncovered.

Chapter 25: Ghost of The Loch

The village was unusually quiet when they arrived, the usual hum of morning activity stifled by something heavier, something unseen. Whispers followed them as they walked, hushed conversations slipping between doorways and over market stalls. Isla kept close to Callum, her eyes scanning the faces of the villagers. Fear was etched into their expressions.

They reached the docks, where a small crowd had gathered near the water's edge. A group of fishermen stood in tight clusters, muttering amongst themselves, while a few women clutched at their shawls, their faces pale.

Callum stepped forward, his presence commanding. "Who saw it first?"

A wiry old man, his hands calloused from years at sea, stepped forward. "Twas Finlay," he said, voice rough as the waves. "He was out late, fixing his nets, when he heard the singing. Said it weren't the wind, nor the waves—it was a woman's voice, clear as day. He called out, but she never answered. Just kept singing. Then the mist rolled in, and when it cleared, she was gone. And now—" He gestured to the water. "So is he."

A murmur rippled through the crowd. Isla wrapped her arms around herself, trying to ward off the creeping chill in her bones. "Has this happened before?" she asked, already knowing the answer.

The old man nodded gravely. "Aye. Not for years, but we remember. It starts with a song. Then the disappearances. Always men. Always the loch."

"And none have ever returned?" Callum asked, his voice even, measured.

A woman clutched a wooden pendant at her throat. "They do…but they are never again the same."

The weight of the words settled over Isla like a heavy cloak. She turned her gaze to the loch. The water was still, too still, the surface like glass reflecting the grey sky above. It was beautiful in an unsettling way, a deceptive calm that masked whatever lay beneath.

"Where was Finlay last seen?" Callum asked.

"His boat was moored just beyond the bend," one of the younger men offered, pointing further along the shore. "We found it drifting this morning, empty. Oars gone, as if they were never there."

Callum turned to Isla, his expression unreadable. "We need to see it."

She nodded, following as they moved away from the gathering, stepping past the line of trees that framed the village. The shore was uneven here, rocks jutting up through the earth, the scent of damp moss and brine heavy in the air. And then she saw it — the boat.

It rocked gently in the shallows, tethered to nothing. The wood was slick with morning dew, its hull empty, untouched. But Isla's gaze was drawn to something else.

Footprints.

Bare, unmistakable, leading from the water's edge up the shore. But they didn't lead away.

They led toward the loch.

Isla's breath caught. "Callum…"

He followed her gaze, his own sharp with understanding. "Someone — or something — walked out of the water."

A gust of wind whipped through the trees, carrying with it the faintest sound.

A melody.

Low, haunting, just on the edge of hearing.

Isla turned to Callum, her heart pounding.

Chapter 26:

Footprints

The melody was faint, a whisper on the wind, but it sent a shiver down Isla's spine. It wasn't the kind of song one heard with their ears alone—it settled into the bones, into the mind, drawing them toward the water with an unspoken invitation.

Callum stiffened beside her, his gaze fixed on the loch.

"Do you hear that?" Isla asked, her voice barely above a breath.

He nodded once. "Aye."

The footprints—they hadn't led away from the shore but back into the water. Someone had emerged from the depths, walked upon the land, and then returned. The realization settled over Isla like a weight, pressing against her chest.

She took a step closer to the boat, her fingers trailing along the damp wood. There was no sign of struggle, no blood, no indication that Finlay had fought. Had he left willingly? Had the song called him, the same way it now wrapped around them like a lure?

"We should go back," Callum said suddenly, his voice edged with something Isla couldn't quite place. Fear? Or something deeper, something unspoken?

But Isla couldn't move. She was staring at the footprints, at the way the last step vanished beneath the lapping water. And then—

A ripple.

It was slight, barely disturbing the surface, but it was there. The loch had been still, unnaturally so, and now something stirred beneath.

"Callum," she whispered, her hand reaching for his.

Another ripple.

A shape moved beneath the water, just beyond where the footprints ended. A shadow, shifting, slow and deliberate.

Isla's breath hitched. The stories had always said the woman had disappeared into the loch, her sorrow binding her to it. But what if that wasn't all? What if she had never left at all?

The melody rose, stronger now, curling around them like mist. Isla swayed slightly before Callum's grip tightened on her hand, grounding her.

"Back. Now," he ordered, his tone leaving no room for argument.

She didn't resist this time. Together, they stepped away from the shore, retreating toward the trees. The song followed them, lingering in the air even as they turned their backs to the water.

But Isla knew, deep in her heart, that the loch was no longer content with whispers. It wanted something.

And it wasn't done calling.

Chapter 27: Ripple Effects

The walk back to the village was silent, but tension crackled between Isla and Callum like a storm on the horizon. The melody still echoed in her mind, lingering long after the last note had faded.

The villagers were waiting when they returned, their eyes heavy with questions they dared not voice.

Callum's grip on Isla's hand tightened before he stepped forward.

"We found the boat," he said, his voice steady. "No sign of Finlay. But there were footprints."

A murmur rippled through the crowd, fear creeping into their hushed voices. The old man who had spoken earlier gave a knowing nod. "Aye. Always the same."

A chill coiled around Isla's spine.

"The loch does not only take," the old man continued, his voice low and grim. "It gives back. But what returns is never what was lost."

A hush settled over the crowd, thick as fog. Isla's mind raced, piecing together fragments of stories she had heard since arriving. The woman who had sung her sorrow into the loch—had she truly been leading men to the water... returning them, but not as they once were?

Callum turned to the gathered villagers. "Has anyone else heard the song before last night? Felt anything strange?"

For a long moment, silence stretched between them. Then, finally, a younger woman stepped forward, hesitant.

"Two nights ago, my husband—he woke in the night, said he heard something outside. He went to look, but there was nothing there. Since then, he hasn't been himself. Says he feels… off."

A heavy stillness followed her words. Callum exhaled sharply, rubbing a hand over his jaw. "Where is he now?"

"At home. Resting. But he barely speaks. Just stares toward the water."

Isla swallowed hard. The pull she had felt at the shore—the lure of the song—was it stronger for the men? Was it already weaving its way through the village, its melody threading through those who had heard it?

She turned to Callum. "We need to see him. Now."

He nodded, taking her hand once more as they followed the woman through the winding village paths. The weight of the loch pressed upon them, unseen but undeniable.

And in the distance, just barely carried by the wind, Isla swore she heard it again.

A song.

Waiting.

Chapter 28: The Brink

The cottage was small, its walls weathered by time and the relentless Highland winds. A single candle flickered inside, casting long shadows through the window as Isla and Callum approached. The woman led them to the door but hesitated before opening it.

"He hasn't spoken much since that night," she whispered. "But when he does… it's not him."

A chill skated down Isla's spine, but she pushed forward, stepping inside.

The air was thick with the scent of damp earth and something else—something faintly metallic. The man sat in a chair near the fireplace, his back to them, unmoving. His shoulders were rigid, his hands resting on his knees. For a moment, Isla wondered if he had even noticed their arrival.

Callum stepped forward cautiously. "Ian?"

The man flinched, his fingers twitching before curling into fists. Slowly, he turned his head. His eyes, once a warm hazel, now carried an eerie sheen, reflecting the firelight with an unnatural glint.

"You shouldn't have come," Ian murmured, his voice rough, almost hollow.

Isla swallowed, exchanging a glance with Callum before stepping closer. "We need to know what happened," she said gently. "Tell us about the song."

Ian's gaze flickered to her, something unreadable passing over his face. Then, he laughed—a low, humorless sound that sent ice through her veins.

"You think you hear it now?" He shook his head. "You don't know what it truly sounds like. Not until it's inside you."

A shudder rippled through Isla.

Ian lifted a hand to his chest as though grasping at something unseen. "It doesn't let go," he whispered. "It doesn't stop."

Callum's jaw tightened. "What doesn't stop?"

Ian's fingers dug into his shirt. "The pull. It's in the blood now." His breath hitched, his entire body tensing. "And she's still waiting."

The candle flickered violently, as if caught in a sudden gust of wind—though the air in the cottage remained deathly still.

Then, Ian's head snapped up. "You should leave. Before she knows you're listening."

Isla's heart pounded.

Callum reached for her hand, pulling her back toward the door. "We've heard enough."

But as they turned to go, Ian spoke again, his voice barely more than a breath—yet it cut through the silence like a blade.

"It's too late."

And from somewhere beyond the walls, just beneath the whisper of the wind, the song began again.

Low. Beckoning.

Calling.

Chapter 29: Gone

The night had deepened by the time Isla and Callum left the cottage, but the village felt far from asleep. A hush blanketed the streets—not the peaceful quiet of a town at rest, but the kind that sat heavy in the air, expectant. Watching.

The wind had picked up, curling through the narrow paths, carrying the distant scent of the loch. And beneath it—just beneath it—Isla swore she could still hear the song, winding its way through the dark like an unseen thread, stretching between them and the water.

Callum pulled her to a stop beneath the glow of a lantern. "What do we do?" His voice was steady, but there was an edge to it, something unspoken lurking beneath his words.

Isla exhaled sharply, her mind racing. "We need to understand it. The stories, the warnings — there has to be something more. Something we've missed."

Callum nodded, his jaw tightening. "The elders. The ones who have lived here the longest. If anyone knows how to stop this, it's them."

A gust of wind sent the flame of the lantern sputtering.

A sharp scream shattered the stillness.

Both of them spun toward the sound — a woman's voice, raw with terror, coming from deeper in the village. Without hesitation, they ran.

The streets blurred past, the wind howling now, as if the loch itself had exhaled. The screaming had stopped by the time they reached the source, but Isla's breath hitched at the sight before them.

The younger woman from earlier — the one whose husband had heard the song—stood at the doorway of her home, her face pale as death. Her hands clutched at the doorframe as if it was the only thing keeping her upright.

Callum reached her first. "What happened?"

She turned wide, glassy eyes toward them. "He's gone."

A sick weight settled in Isla's stomach. "Gone?"

She gave a shuddering breath, her fingers trembling as she lifted her hand to point—past the house, past the winding path, toward the open fields beyond. Toward the loch.

"He just... walked away," she whispered. "Didn't speak. Didn't look back. He just walked."

Isla stepped forward, peering past the house. The moon had broken through the clouds, casting a pale glow over the land. And there — cutting through the damp earth, unmistakable in their direction — were footprints.

Leading straight to the water.

The loch had called again.

But this time, they could still stop it.

Isla and Callum exchanged a look before breaking into a sprint, following the footprints before the loch could claim another soul.

The melody, soft as a sigh, curled through the air once more.

And the loch waited.

Chapter 30: Trance

The night had never felt so vast, so alive.

Isla and Callum ran, their breath sharp in the cold air, their feet pounding against the damp earth. The path twisted through the village, narrowing as it neared the fields, but Isla barely registered the terrain beneath her. Her focus was on the footprints stretching ahead, leading straight to the loch.

"He can't have gotten far," Callum panted. "The song—"

"I know," Isla cut in, urgency pressing against her ribs. "We need to hurry."

The loch loomed ahead, dark and endless beneath the moonlight. The air was thick with something unseen, a pull stronger than mere curiosity, an ancient whisper threading through the wind.

Then she saw him.

Ian stood at the water's edge, the lake lapping at his boots. His posture was eerily still, his head tilted slightly, as if listening to something just beyond reach. The reflection of the moon shimmered on the surface, distorting as if something beneath stirred.

"Ian!" Isla called out.

No response.

Callum surged forward, but Isla grabbed his arm. "Wait," she whispered. "If he's in a trance, we can't just startle him."

Her mind raced, recalling the stories, the legends. If the song had a hold on him, simply dragging him back might not be enough. He had to wake from it. He had to resist.

"Ian!" she tried again, her voice softer this time. "Can you hear me?"

A flicker—just the slightest movement in his fingers.

Callum took a step forward, his voice steady but firm. "Ian, it's Callum. Your wife is waiting for you. She's terrified."

The wind shifted. The melody swirled around them, insistent, beckoning.

Ian took another step forward. Water soaked into his boots. His hands twitched.

Panic clawed at Isla's throat. Think. Think.

Then she did the only thing she could think of. She reached out, grabbing his hand, and squeezed hard. "Ian," she said, her voice fierce. "Come back."

His body jerked. A breath caught in his throat. For a moment, she swore she saw something flicker in his eyes, like a man teetering on the edge of wakefulness.

Callum clapped a hand on his shoulder. "Fight it, Ian."

A long beat of silence stretched between them.

Then Ian inhaled sharply, staggering back as if he had been yanked from the depths of a dream. He blinked wildly, his chest heaving. "I... I was..." His gaze darted to the loch, then to them, horror dawning in his eyes. "Gods above. I almost—"

Callum steadied him. "You're alright. We got you."

Ian shuddered, running a shaking hand through his hair. "The song… it was inside my head. I couldn't—" His voice broke. "It wanted me to follow."

Isla exchanged a glance with Callum. "This is getting worse."

Callum nodded grimly. "We need answers. Now."

Ian swallowed hard, glancing back toward the village. "The elders," he murmured. "They know more than they let on."

Isla straightened. "Then it's time we found them."

The loch was silent now, but the air still hummed with something unseen.

Watching.

Waiting.

Chapter 31: The Elders

The elders' cottage was dimly lit, the scent of peat smoke curling through the air. The three elders sat in a semi-circle, their faces carved with time and knowledge, their eyes shadowed by the weight of what they knew. Isla and Callum stood before them, tension crackling between them like a storm ready to break.

The eldest of the three, a man with deep-set eyes and a voice like rustling leaves, gestured for them to sit. "You have seen what the loch can do. You have felt its call. Now you wish to know how to stop it."

Isla swallowed hard. "Yes."

The second elder, her hair lined with grey and pulled back in a braid, leaned forward. "The song is not merely sound. It is a tether. A thread woven through time, binding those who hear it to the loch itself. Some resist. Others do not."

Callum exhaled sharply, running a hand through his hair. "Then how do we break it? How do we stop it before it takes anyone else?"

The third elder, silent until now, lifted his gaze. His eyes—sharp and piercing—locked onto Isla's. "It does not call to just anyone. It seeks those with longing. Those with sorrow.

Those who ache for something they cannot name."

Isla's breath hitched. She thought of the pull she had felt, the way the melody had wrapped around her heart, whispering promises she couldn't quite grasp. It had nearly taken her, just as it had taken Ian, just as it had taken countless others before him.

The eldest elder shifted in his chair, the firelight casting deep lines across his face. "The song is not of this time. It was born long ago, when grief was given form, when loss refused to be silent. The woman who sang her sorrow into the loch — we do not know her name. But we know she waits. And she will keep waiting."

A chill slithered down Isla's spine. "Then we need to find her. If she is the one who calls them, she is the one who must be stopped."

A heavy silence followed. Then, finally, the second elder nodded. "Aye. But finding her is not the challenge. It is what must be done once you do."

Isla and Callum exchanged a glance, the weight of the moment pressing against them. Callum set his jaw, his hand brushing against Isla's, grounding her.

"Tell us what we need to do."

Chapter 32: Unbound

The fire crackled low in the hearth, the shadows of the elders shifting with its flickering light. The weight of their words lingered, wrapping around Isla and Callum like an unseen force.

The eldest elder leaned forward, his fingers interlocking as he studied them. "To stop the song, you must face the one who sings it. She lingers between this world and the next, bound by grief, by longing. You must unbind her."

Isla's throat tightened. "Unbind her how?"

The second elder, the woman with the silver-streaked braid, exhaled. "She is tethered to the loch by sorrow. You must find what keeps her bound, and you must give her peace."

Callum scoffed softly, shaking his head. "And if she doesn't want peace? If she's been here for centuries, luring people to madness—what if she doesn't stop?"

The third elder, silent until now, spoke with quiet certainty. "Then she must be forced to let go."

A shiver ran down Isla's spine. "And how do we do that?"

The eldest elder's gaze was heavy, unyielding. "That is for you to discover. But know this—she is strongest in the place where she first sang her sorrow. The loch will not give her up easily. And neither will she."

A heavy silence settled between them. Isla's pulse thundered in her ears. The thought of standing before the woman—before the spirit who had haunted the loch for generations—sent an ache of dread curling in her stomach. But beneath it, woven into the fear, was something else.

Determination.

She felt Callum shift beside her, his warmth grounding her against the cold reality of what lay ahead. When she met his eyes, there was no hesitation there, no doubt. Only unwavering resolve.

And something more.

Something unspoken, humming between them like the call of the loch itself.

The elders stood as one, signaling the conversation had ended. "Go now," the woman murmured. "You do not have much time. The song will not wait forever."

Callum's hand found Isla's as they stepped outside. The night air was sharp, the village silent around them. The loch loomed beyond the fields, a dark, endless expanse that stretched toward the horizon. Waiting.

Isla exhaled, feeling the tension coil inside her, threatening to unravel. "We need a plan. We can't just walk into this blind."

Callum's thumb brushed over the back of her hand, a fleeting touch that sent a shiver through her. "Then let's figure it out. Together."

She looked up at him, her pulse thrumming, not just from fear, but from something deeper, something undeniable. The space between them felt fragile, stretched taut with unspoken words, with everything they had held back for too long.

She didn't know who moved first, only that suddenly, she was pressed against him, his warmth chasing away the chill. His hands framed her face, his breath fanning across her lips, hesitation warring with need in his eyes.

"Isla—"

She silenced him with a kiss, desperate, searching. The world faded, the loch, the song, the fear—none of it mattered in that moment. Only this. Only him. Only the fire between them that had been waiting to burn.

Callum groaned against her lips, his grip tightening, pulling her closer. She melted into him, her fingers tangling in his hair, losing herself in the storm they had become.

When they finally broke apart, breathless, foreheads pressed together, Isla whispered, "Together. No matter what comes next."

Callum's grip on her waist tightened. "Aye. Together."

The loch still waited, the melody still curled at the edges of the night. But for the first time, Isla didn't feel its pull alone.

They would face it. Together.

Chapter 33: Lost Souls

The journey to the abandoned cottage was silent but thick with tension. The night air was crisp, the distant call of the loch ever-present, weaving through the trees like an unseen force. Isla walked beside Callum, her heart pounding with a mix of anticipation and unease. They had spent the night tangled in each other, surrendering to the heat between them, but there was no mistaking the weight of what lay ahead.

The cottage loomed before them, its stone walls weathered by time, half-consumed by ivy and the creeping embrace of nature. It stood as a relic of a love lost to sorrow, its history whispering through the crumbling mortar. Callum pushed open the door, the wood groaning in protest. The air inside was stale, thick with dust and memories that didn't belong to them.

Isla moved forward, her fingers brushing along the remnants of a life once lived. A table, its surface marred with age, stood in the center of the room. Two chairs lay toppled beside it. On a nearby shelf, books sat untouched, their spines brittle with time. Callum knelt beside the hearth, shifting through the charred remains of what had once been a fire.

"It feels like a place for lost souls," Isla murmured, wrapping her arms around herself.

Callum exhaled. "Aye. But maybe it holds the answers we need."

She nodded, her gaze sweeping the room until it landed on an old chest half-buried beneath a fallen beam. Heart hammering, she moved toward it, brushing away the dust before prying it open. Inside, wrapped in delicate linen, was a leather-bound journal.

She carefully lifted it, fingers trembling as she unfastened the brittle clasp. Callum came to stand behind her, his warmth seeping into her as she opened to the first page. The ink had faded, but the words remained legible, a desperate, aching script etched onto the fragile parchment.

A cruel hand stole his life, stole our future, and left him in the water, alone in the dark. The man they forced upon me, the one I refused, could not bear to see me love another. He took his revenge in the blackest of ways, with blood and steel, and cast the only man I ever loved into the depths of the loch. His body is there still. And so I wait. I tether my soul to the water, to him. I sing so that one day, our love might live again. That we might find each other once more.

Isla felt her pulse throb in her throat. "He was murdered," she breathed. "The man she was supposed to marry killed him."

Callum exhaled sharply, his fingers flexing at his sides. "And she bound herself to the loch, to him, so they would never be apart."

A sick sort of understanding settled over Isla. The lullaby — it was not just a call, not just grief. It was love twisted by sorrow, a love so deep and unrelenting that it had refused to die.

And now, it claimed others, pulling them into its endless yearning.

She turned the last page, the ink fainter now, like a whisper in the dark.

Only love can set me free. The love we were denied. A love that was meant to be.

Isla's breath trembled as she met Callum's gaze. "We are the key."

Callum's throat bobbed as he swallowed, his eyes dark and searching. "Isla—"

Further along, the ink was darker, the handwriting erratic, trembling with madness.

I cannot bear it. The loch sings to me, whispers of him, and I go willingly. If I cannot have him in this life, then I will find him in the water. I will not fight it anymore. I will be his again.

A sickening chill rolled down Isla's spine. "She let it take her."

Callum's fingers brushed against her wrist. "She gave herself to it."

The revelation hung between them, a dark, tragic truth that mirrored their own unspoken fears. Love so strong it could destroy. Need so powerful it could consume. Isla turned to Callum, her pulse hammering.

"She didn't get to finish her story," she whispered. "She didn't get her happy ending."

Callum's eyes darkened, something raw burning behind them. "But we still can."

The final words in the journal burned into Isla's mind.

The love that was stolen must be reborn. Only two souls bound by fate, by passion, by the very same fire we carried, can set me free. If they find what we lost, if they live as we could not, the chains will break, and I will finally rest.

Isla's heart pounded. "It's us, Callum. It has to be us."

His fingers tightened around hers, his expression unreadable but intense. "Then we won't let history repeat itself."

The weight of it—the danger, the uncertainty, the desperate, aching need—drove her forward. She reached for him, fingers tangling in the fabric of his shirt as she pulled him close. He caught her waist, his grip firm, claiming, and then his mouth was on hers.

It was fire and desperation, a clash of teeth and tongues, a need that eclipsed reason. Callum pressed her back against the wall, hands roaming, fingers seeking, unraveling her with every touch. The air between them burned, thick with want, with something deeper—something neither of them dared to name.

His hands skimmed the curve of her hips, slipping beneath the hem of her shirt, tracing the heated skin beneath. Isla gasped against his lips, arching into him, the journal slipping from her fingers, forgotten as his body pressed against hers. There was no hesitation, no restraint—only raw, unfiltered need.

Callum broke away, his breath ragged, his forehead resting against hers. "Tell me you want this," he rasped.

She met his gaze, her body trembling, not from fear but from everything he made her feel. "I don't just want it," she whispered. "I need it."

That was all it took.

He lifted her effortlessly, her legs wrapping around his waist as he carried her to the worn mattress in the corner of the room. They collapsed onto it in a tangle of limbs, hands desperate, mouths searching. Clothes became an afterthought, lost to the fervor of touch and taste.

Callum's lips trailed down her throat, his teeth grazing the sensitive skin, drawing a gasp from her as his hands explored, memorized. Isla arched beneath him, nails digging into his shoulders, pulling him closer, urging him on.

There was nothing soft about this. It was urgent, primal, a consuming fire that neither of them wanted to extinguish. Every touch was a promise, every moan a confession, every breath a vow.

And when they finally came together, it was like lightning striking the earth—hot, unstoppable, electric.

After, as they lay tangled in the aftermath, the only sound was their ragged breathing and the crackling of the dying fire. Callum brushed his fingers over Isla's damp skin, his lips pressing lazy kisses to her shoulder.

"We will finish the story," he murmured against her skin. "We will end this curse."

Isla turned her head, meeting his gaze, her body still thrumming from everything they had shared. "Together."

He smiled, slow and wicked. "Aye, mo chridhe. Together."

Chapter 34: Love That Was Meant To Be

The air in the cottage was thick with the remnants of passion and the weight of revelation. The fire had burned low, casting flickering shadows along the crumbling walls, but Isla and Callum had long since abandoned sleep. The truth of the past, the burden of the love that had been stolen, lay between them like an unspoken vow.

Isla sat up, the old sheet slipping from her bare skin, exposing the marks Callum had left upon her — evidence of a hunger that neither of them could contain. Her pulse still thrummed with the aftermath, but her mind was restless, tangled in the echoes of the journal's final words.

Only love can set me free. The love we were denied. A love that was meant to be.

She traced her fingers over the ink, the parchment cool beneath her touch. "It has to be us," she murmured, more to herself than to Callum. "We are the love that was meant to be."

Callum shifted beside her, the heat of his body a grounding force. His hand skimmed along her spine, a slow, possessive touch that sent a shiver cascading through her. "Aye, mo chridhe. There's no doubt now. We were always meant to be here — to finish what was left undone."

A weight settled over her chest, heavy with purpose. "Then we can't run from this," she whispered, turning to face him. His gaze locked onto hers, dark and unwavering. "We have to see it through."

Callum exhaled slowly, his fingers threading through her hair before cupping the nape of her neck. "And we will. But not tonight." His voice was rough, edged with something primal. "Tonight, I need you. Just you."

The words sent a delicious tremor through her. He had claimed her before, but this was different. This was not just need—it was possession, devotion, a vow sealed not in words but in touch, in breath, in the fire that ignited between them.

Callum moved swiftly, rolling her beneath him, his weight pressing her into the ancient mattress. His hands were everywhere at once—mapping her, memorizing her, worshipping every inch as if she were something sacred. Isla arched into him, gasping as his mouth found the sensitive spot just below her ear, his teeth grazing over her skin.

"You feel this?" he murmured against her throat, his voice thick with desire. "This is fate, Isla. This is us reclaiming what was stolen, and something more."

She could only nod, her fingers digging into his shoulders as he descended, his lips tracing a searing path down her body. Every touch was a declaration, every whisper a promise. The air crackled around them, thick with heat and something else—something older than time itself.

By the time he finally sank into her, she was lost, consumed by him, by them. It was not just bodies coming together—it was souls colliding, past and present intertwining in a way that felt inevitable. Every thrust, every gasp, every broken moan was a piece of history rewriting itself, righting the wrongs that had been done.

The fire within them burned long into the night, until exhaustion finally claimed them. And even then, as Isla lay wrapped in Callum's arms, the steady beat of his heart beneath her palm, she knew without a doubt—

They were the key. And their love would change everything.

Chapter 35: The Key

The wind howled through the trees as Isla and Callum made their way back to the loch, their footsteps quiet against the damp earth. The night was thick with tension, charged with something unseen but deeply felt. The revelation from the journal still echoed between them, not as a question, but as undeniable truth.

They were the key.

The loch stretched before them, dark and endless, the water lapping gently at the shore as if whispering secrets only they could understand. Isla could feel it—something shifting, something waiting. The weight of history pressed against her chest, but it no longer felt suffocating. Instead, it felt like destiny pulling her forward.

Callum reached for her hand, threading his fingers through hers. "It's always been us," he murmured.

Isla turned to him, searching his face. There was no fear there, no doubt. Just certainty. Just him. The warmth of his touch steadied her, anchored her in the storm of everything they had discovered. And yet, beneath the gravity of what lay ahead, there was something else—something burning between them, undeniable and consuming.

She didn't fight it. She never had.

Their love had grown in the spaces between danger and discovery, in whispered confessions and stolen moments. It had been forged in fire, in the pull of fate and the promise of something bigger than themselves. And now, standing on the edge of something they could not yet see but knew was coming, it only burned brighter.

Callum cupped her face, his thumb tracing the curve of her cheek. "No more waiting," he said, his voice rough with emotion. "We finish this together."

Isla's breath hitched, her pulse a frantic drum beneath her skin. "Together," she whispered.

Then he kissed her, and the world around them ceased to exist. There was no loch, no curse, no centuries of sorrow. There was only the fire between them, the heat of his hands as they slid down her back, pulling her closer. The taste of him, the way he breathed her in like she was something sacred.

They fell into each other, lost in the inevitability of them. Their bodies pressed together, urgency giving way to something deeper, something that spoke of forever. Callum's hands mapped her skin like he was memorizing every inch of her, his touch reverent, unyielding.

"I love you," he breathed against her lips, the words an oath, a promise.

Isla's heart clenched, her eyes burning with the force of it. "I love you too," she answered, and it was everything.

The loch whispered, the wind carried their names, but nothing mattered except the way they fit together, as if the universe itself had been waiting for this moment. For them.

When the dawn broke, they would be ready.

For whatever came next.

Chapter 36: Specter

The night was alive with whispers. The loch churned under the moon's silver light, the water lapping at the shore in rhythmic pulses, as if breathing with the weight of history. Isla and Callum stood at the edge, their hands entwined, the journal pressed between them like a tether to the past. The truth had been laid bare—the woman's sorrow, her love lost to jealousy and cruelty, her soul bound to the loch, waiting for a love strong enough to break the cycle. Their love.

The revelation sat heavy in Isla's chest, not as fear, but as something inevitable. They had been drawn together, guided by unseen hands, their passion igniting like dry kindling. Every moment, every touch, every whispered confession had been leading them here.

She turned to Callum, his face shadowed yet striking in the moonlight. His eyes burned with purpose, his grip on her tightening, not out of fear, but possession. He would not let her go. They had come too far, endured too much.

"She's waiting," Isla murmured. "For us."

Callum cupped her face, his thumb tracing the curve of her cheek. "Aye, mo chridhe. And we'll see her free."

A shiver raced down Isla's spine — not from the cold, but from the intensity of his gaze. This man, this storm of a man, was hers. The truth of it settled deep, deeper than even the loch's dark secrets.

They moved in sync, stepping into the shallows, the icy water curling around their ankles. The song was there, woven into the ripples, vibrating through the very air around them. It was a melody of longing, of endless waiting, a song of love that refused to die. And Isla answered.

Her voice rose, soft at first, trembling with emotion, then stronger, fuller. She sang the lullaby as it was meant to be sung—not a dirge of sorrow, but a promise, a vow. Callum's voice joined hers, their harmonies weaving together, binding them to the past, to the woman who had waited so long. The wind howled in response, the loch stirring, the reflection of the moon shattering against the restless waves.

The air thickened, charged with something ancient, something watching.

Then, she appeared.

The ghostly figure rose from the water, her form ethereal, her sorrowful eyes locked onto them. The weight of centuries clung to her, but there was something else now — hope. She reached out, her hands trembling, her lips parting as if to speak, but the words never came. Instead, the loch surged, waves crashing around Isla and Callum, the water reaching, pulling, demanding.

Callum grabbed Isla, anchoring her against him. "Hold on to me," he commanded.

She clung to him as the water swirled higher, wrapping around their waists. The spirit's eyes darted between them, recognition dawning, the shattered pieces of her love finding their place. A new verse of the lullaby formed on Isla's lips, words she had never known yet felt as though they had always been hers. She sang them into the night, and the spirit gasped, as if breathing for the first time in centuries.

Light erupted from the loch, golden and blinding, the force of it sending shockwaves through the water. The spirit's expression softened, her features illuminated with something beyond sorrow — peace. The moment stretched, time folding in on itself, past and present converging.

Then, with a final, shuddering breath, she faded, dissolving into the wind, her essence scattering like embers into the night.

The loch stilled. The song ended.

Isla sagged against Callum, her body trembling. He held her close, his lips pressing against her temple, his breath warm against her skin.

"It's done," he murmured.

She looked up at him, heart thundering. "We did it."

A slow, knowing smile tugged at his lips. "Aye, mo chridhe. Together."

And then he kissed her, the taste of triumph and love sealing their fate, their passion burning brighter than the stars overhead.

Chapter 37: Free

The loch had quieted, its surface as smooth as glass, the restless energy of the past settled at last. The air was thick with something unspoken, a hum of power still lingering, but softer now—like a lullaby that had finally found its resolution. The woman's spirit was free, and with her release, something within Isla and Callum had shifted, deepened.

Callum's arms remained firm around Isla, his breath warm against her temple. He hadn't loosened his hold since the moment the loch had gone still, as if unwilling to let her go. Not that she wanted him to. She turned in his embrace, her hands resting against his chest, feeling the steady, grounding rhythm of his heartbeat beneath her palm.

"It's over," she whispered, the words curling into the space between them.

His gaze held hers, steady and sure. "Aye, but we are only beginning."

Her heart swelled, her body thrumming with something more than the adrenaline of what they had just done. It was a feeling that had been growing steadily between them, nurtured in stolen moments, in whispered confessions, in nights spent tangled together, exploring the depths of what they had found in each other. There had never been denial, only inevitability.

Callum reached up, brushing a damp strand of hair from her cheek. The way he looked at her—like she was the most precious thing he had ever held—made heat pool low in her belly. She pressed closer, her fingers curling into the fabric of his shirt.

"We should go back," she murmured, but there was no urgency in her voice.

Callum's lips curved. "In a moment."

The moon bathed them in silver, the loch stretching behind them like a mirror of the heavens. The world felt hushed, reverent. As if it, too, was waiting for what came next.

He lifted a hand to cradle the back of her head, his fingers threading into her hair. The kiss that followed was slow, unhurried, deep. A claiming. A promise. Isla melted into it, into him, the sensation unraveling every thread of tension that had wound tight through her body. He kissed her as though he had all the time in the world — and for the first time since she had arrived, she believed they did.

When they finally pulled apart, her breath came fast, her hands shaking slightly as she traced the strong line of his jaw. He caught one of them, bringing it to his lips, his eyes dark with something she knew mirrored in her own.

"We should go," he admitted, though he made no move to release her.

She nodded, but still, they lingered a moment longer, unwilling to break the spell.

The walk back to the cottage was different. The weight of the past no longer clung to them like a ghost. The night air was crisp, scented with heather and damp earth, and Isla found herself reaching for Callum's hand without thinking. He took it immediately, linking their fingers, his thumb brushing over her skin in an absent caress that sent warmth curling through her.

When they reached the cottage, the fire had burned low, the embers casting a golden glow across the room. Isla turned to Callum, searching his face, seeing the same unspoken words reflected back at her.

"Stay with me tonight," she said softly, though they both knew it was not a question. He had not left her bed since the first time he had come to her, and she didn't want to wake without him beside her.

A slow, knowing smile touched his lips. "Always."

And when he pulled her into his arms, lifting her with ease, Isla wrapped herself around him, letting herself be carried deeper into the night, into him, into everything they were becoming.

Chapter 38:

Aftermath

The loch lay silent in the aftermath, its once-restless waters now smooth as glass, reflecting the stars above like a portal to another world. The air still hummed with something ancient, something powerful, but there was no longer a presence lingering — only the echoes of what had been, of what had finally found peace.

Along the edge of the loch on a patch of lush green grass, Isla remained in Callum's arms, her body pressed against his, still trembling from the weight of what they had done. Her heart thundered in her chest, but it was not fear that gripped her. It was him. The feel of him, the warmth of him, the undeniable truth of him. He was her anchor in this storm of fate, and she had never felt more certain of anything in her life.

Callum's fingers skimmed the damp strands of her hair, his touch gentle despite the strength that ran through him. "You're shakin'," he murmured, his voice a low rasp against her ear.

She let out a breath she hadn't realized she was holding, tilting her face to meet his gaze. His eyes burned with something deeper than triumph — something raw and unguarded. Love. It was there, woven into the way he held her, into the way he looked at her as if she were the only thing in this world worth holding onto.

"I'm not afraid," she whispered, reaching up to touch his jaw, rough from the stubble that had grown over their days entangled in this journey. "I'm just...feeling everything all at once."

His lips curved, the ghost of a smile touching the corner of his mouth before he leaned in, brushing his lips over hers. It was not a claiming—it was not a desperate grasping. It was something deeper. A promise, sealed in the quiet between them.

She melted into him, her hands sliding up his chest, feeling the steady thrum of his heartbeat beneath her fingertips. The moments they had stolen together, the nights spent tangled in sheets, the whispered confessions in the dark—they had not been fleeting. They had been building toward this, toward something unbreakable.

Callum pulled her closer, until there was no space left between them. "I meant what I said," he murmured against her lips. "We did this together. I could never have done it without you."

She shook her head, her forehead pressing to his. "We were always meant to do this."

The truth of it settled between them. The loch, the woman, the echoes of love and sorrow that had shaped their journey—it had all led to this moment. To them.

A breeze stirred around them, soft and warm, as if the very land itself had exhaled in relief. The stars above seemed to shine brighter, the weight of the past no longer pressing upon the night.

Callum lifted his head, his gaze sweeping over the loch one last time before returning to her. "Come," he said, threading his fingers through hers. "Let's go home."

Home.

The word struck something deep within her. Not because it was a place, but because of who she was with. Wherever he was, that was home.

She nodded, letting him lead her away from the water's edge, away from the past that had held them captive. Toward the future they would build together.

Toward love that would never be bound by time again.

Chapter 39: Home

The morning sun broke through the mist, golden light spilling over the hills, casting the loch in a shimmering embrace. Isla stirred, her body tucked against Callum's warmth, the steady rhythm of his breath grounding her in the reality of all that had transpired. The loch was calm now, its surface smooth as glass, reflecting the sky with an eerie sort of peace. The storm of the night before had passed, but its weight lingered in the air between them.

Callum shifted beside her, his arm tightening instinctively around her waist, drawing her closer. She smiled against his bare skin, pressing a lingering kiss to his shoulder, savoring the quiet, the stillness of a world that had, for a time, been chaos. They had freed her — the woman bound to the loch, her sorrow carried away by the lullaby Isla had sung with every piece of her soul. And now, they were here, in the aftermath of history rewritten, of love tested and proven unbreakable.

Callum's fingers traced slow, languid patterns along her spine. "Yer quiet this morning, lass."

She exhaled, tilting her head to meet his gaze. "I'm just... taking it all in. Everything that's happened, everything we've done."

His expression softened, and he cupped her face, his thumb brushing over her cheek. "Aye. We've been through the fire, you and I. But we came out the other side, stronger than before."

She turned into his touch, pressing a kiss to his palm. "It doesn't feel real yet. That she's gone. That we broke the cycle."

"It's real," he murmured, his lips ghosting over her forehead. "And it's over."

She closed her eyes, letting his reassurance settle deep in her bones. But even as relief coursed through her, there was something else beneath it — a sense of change, of an ending that inevitably signaled a new beginning. The loch had released its hold on the past, but what did that mean for them? For her?

Callum must have sensed her hesitation, because he shifted, rolling her beneath him with effortless ease. His weight, his warmth, his presence—all of it anchored her in the now. "Tell me what's goin' on in that head of yours."

She hesitated, biting her lip. "What happens now? We came here because of the journal, because of the loch. Now that it's over, do we just... go back?"

He studied her, his gaze dark, unwavering. "Do you want to go back?"

The question lingered between them, heavy with unspoken truths. She had come here searching for something—adventure, purpose, maybe even herself. And in Callum, she had found all of it. But what if he didn't see it the same way? What if this was only meant to be a fleeting chapter in the grander story of her life?

She swallowed hard. "I don't know where I belong anymore."

Callum's expression darkened, something fierce and possessive flickering behind his eyes. "You belong with me."

Her breath caught, the certainty in his words wrapping around her like a vow. "Callum—"

"I mean it, Isla." His voice was rough, raw. "This isn't just a moment for me. You're not just a passing storm. You're the goddamn sky. And I'll be damned if I let you think otherwise."

Emotion swelled in her chest, too big, too consuming. She reached for him, pulling him down, her lips finding his in a kiss that spoke of love, of promises yet to be made but already written in their souls. He met her with the same desperation, the same need, as if proving through touch what words could never fully express.

This was home.

Chapter 40: Grandfather's Cottage

The morning mist clung to the hills as Isla and Callum stood before the old stone cottage, its weathered walls steeped in history. The scent of damp earth and heather filled the air, and for a long moment, they simply took it in—the place that had once belonged to Callum's grandfather, the place that had unknowingly waited for them.

"This house… my grandfather's cottage… it should be ours."

Isla stilled, her heart skipping. "Ours?"

He turned to her, a small, knowing smile tugging at his lips. "Aye. This place was always meant to be more than just a piece of my past. It led me to you. I know we spent most of our nights at your cottage, and that place will always hold something sacred between us… but this—" he gestured around them, his voice thick with emotion, "—this is where we build our future."

She exhaled, her fingers curling into his shirt as warmth spread through her chest. She had spent so many nights wrapped in him, tangled in soft sheets in the quiet solitude of her own cottage, their love blooming in the stolen moments between uncertainty and fate. But this place… this had been the beginning of something even greater.

Callum cupped her face, his forehead pressing against hers. "It feels like home. It is home."

Tears pricked at her eyes, but they weren't sad. They were full—full of love, of promise, of the life they were stepping into together.

A gust of wind stirred the trees, carrying the distant chime of bells from the village below. Isla smiled softly. "We should go. The village will be waiting."

Together, they made their way down the winding path, the loch glistening under the morning sun. As they reached the heart of the village, familiar faces turned toward them, eyes widening with recognition and something deeper—relief.

Old Mrs. MacGregor was the first to step forward, her gnarled hands trembling as she clasped Isla's. "The loch… it's different now. There's a peace I've not felt in years."

Callum nodded, his grip on Isla's hand tightening. "It's over. The sorrow that bound it—it's been set free."

Murmurs rippled through the gathered crowd, tears glistening in more than one pair of eyes. But before anyone could speak, a sudden shout rang through the square.

"Finlay!"

The name sent a shiver down Isla's spine, and she turned just as a figure emerged from the edge of the village. Finlay, the fisherman who had vanished without a trace, stood there, his eyes hazy as if waking from a long dream.

"God above," someone whispered. "It's him. He's alive."

Finlay blinked, glancing around at the stunned faces. "I… I don't know what happened," he admitted, voice rough with confusion. "One moment, I was by the loch, and then… nothing. Just a whisper in the dark, holding me in place. And now I'm here."

Isla's breath hitched, her fingers threading through Callum's. The loch had held him, just as it had held so many stories before. But with the spirit freed, the past had loosened its grip.

Mrs. MacGregor clutched her chest, eyes brimming with tears. "It's a miracle."

Callum stepped forward, resting a hand on Finlay's shoulder. "It's a new beginning."

And as Isla looked around at the village — the people, the life, the future that stretched before them — she knew with unwavering certainty that their own new beginning had only just begun.

Chapter 41: The Return

The morning air carried a crispness that hinted at the coming autumn as Isla and Callum lingered in the village square. The people had begun to gather around Finlay, their voices weaving between astonishment and relief. Some clasped his hands, others merely stared, as if afraid he might vanish again like mist over the loch.

Finlay himself looked bewildered, running a hand through his chestnut and gold sunkissed hair. "I still can't make sense of it," he admitted. "I remember feeling as though something had taken hold of me, kept me from moving forward or back. But there was no fear, no pain... just waiting. And now I'm here."

Mrs. MacGregor wiped at her eyes with the corner of her shawl. "The loch had you, lad. But it's let you go now. We all felt it."

Callum nodded, his gaze meeting Isla's before turning back to the crowd. "The spirit that lingered over the waters—she's been freed. Whatever hold the past had on this place, it's been lifted."

A hush fell over the villagers, their expressions shifting from shock to quiet reverence. A few murmured prayers, others exchanged looks filled with unspoken understanding.

Isla swallowed, her fingers tightening around Callum's. "This village has carried so much sorrow. But now, maybe it's time for something new."

A voice rang out from the back of the group. "And what of you two? Will you be staying?" It was one of the old villagers, his eyes sharp with curiosity.

Callum turned slightly, glancing at Isla before answering. "Aye. We will. My grandfather's cottage—it's ours now."

There was a beat of silence, then a wave of murmurs swept through the crowd, voices brimming with approval.

"Good. This village needs you," Mrs. MacGregor said firmly. "And so do we."

A warmth spread through Isla's chest, settling deep in her bones. This place, these people—they had become part of her. And more than that, she had found something here she hadn't even known she was searching for. A home. A future. A love that anchored her in a way nothing else ever had.

Callum pulled her closer, pressing a kiss to her temple before speaking again. "We want to do more than stay. We want to rebuild, to breathe new life into what's been lost. The loch, the village... all of it deserves a new beginning."

A round of murmured agreement swept through the crowd, and Isla could see the way hope flickered to life in their faces. This was more than a homecoming—it was a promise.

As the village slowly began to return to its usual rhythm, Callum and Isla made their way back toward the cottage. The path was familiar now, the land stretching out before them like an unspoken vow.

Callum's voice was quiet when he finally spoke. "Are you ready for this?"

Isla smiled, slipping her fingers between his. "With you? Always."

And as they stepped over the threshold of their new home, the loch glistening behind them in the golden light of morning, they knew — this was just the beginning.

Chapter 42: Together, Always

The first signs of autumn painted the Highlands in gold and amber as Isla and Callum settled into their new home. The stone cottage, worn by time yet sturdy as ever, stood as a testament to the past while holding the promise of their future.

The days that followed were filled with quiet moments and meaningful work. Together, they cleared the overgrown garden, repaired the wooden beams inside, and breathed life back into the home Callum's grandfather had once cherished. There was something deeply satisfying about the labor, knowing they were not only rebuilding a house but forging a life within its walls.

One evening, as the fire crackled in the hearth, Isla stood at the window, gazing out at the loch. The water was still, bathed in moonlight, no longer carrying the whispers of sorrow that once lingered in its depths. A sense of peace settled over her.

Callum stepped behind her, wrapping his arms around her waist. "Ye look lost in thought."

She leaned back into him, exhaling softly. "It's strange, isn't it? How a place can feel like home so suddenly, as if it was always meant to be."

He pressed a kiss to her temple. "Aye. But I think our hearts knew it before our minds did."

She turned in his embrace, looking up at him. "And what does your heart know now?"

He studied her for a long moment, the flickering light of the fire dancing in his eyes. "That I never want to spend another night without ye by my side. That whatever comes next, we face it together."

Emotion swelled in her chest, and she lifted onto her toes, capturing his lips in a slow, lingering kiss. When they parted, she whispered, "Together. Always."

The following morning, the village buzzed with new energy. The return of Finlay, the lifting of the loch's sorrow—everything had shifted, and Isla could feel it in the air. People smiled more, spoke of plans for the future. It was as if the land itself had taken a deep breath and exhaled, ready to move forward.

As Isla and Callum walked through the village square, they were met with warm greetings and approving nods. It was Mrs. MacGregor who stopped them first, her eyes twinkling with mischief. "I hear ye've been makin' that old cottage livable again."

Callum nodded. "Aye."

She clasped her hands together. "Good. This place has been waitin' for a love strong enough to fill it again. And ye two? A perfect fit."

Isla smiled, touched by the words. "We want to do more than just stay. We want to be part of this village, help however we can."

The old woman nodded approvingly. "Then ye'll do just fine."

As the day wore on, Isla and Callum found themselves wrapped in conversations of what was to come — festivals to plan, repairs to be made, futures to build. And with each passing moment, Isla knew one thing with unwavering certainty: they were exactly where they were meant to be.

That night, as they lay entwined beneath the soft blankets of their bed, Isla traced patterns along Callum's arm, her heart full. "What do you think the future holds for us?"

He tightened his hold around her, his voice a gentle rumble in the dark. "Whatever it is, lass, we'll write it together."

And as sleep pulled them under, the wind whispered through the trees, carrying the promise of a new dawn.

Epilogue

The wind whispered over the loch, carrying the scent of rain-kissed earth and wild heather. The water, once haunted by sorrow, now shimmered in the late afternoon light, reflecting the sky in hues of soft gold and deep blue. It was peaceful here—no longer bound by the echoes of the past, but embraced by the love and life that had flourished in its place. They had been wed there as soon as winter had passed, it had only seemed fitting-after all it is where it all began.

Isla stood at the water's edge, her fingers laced with Callum's, the warmth of his palm grounding her as the gentle curve of her belly pressed against the fabric of her dress. She let out a breath, slow and steady, as she watched the ripples dance across the loch's surface.

"We made it," she murmured, tilting her head to rest against his shoulder.

Callum's arm came around her, his touch familiar and steady. "Aye, love. We did."

A year had passed since the loch had finally let go of its ghosts, since they had chosen to make this place their home. And what a home it had become. The village, once weighed down by grief and whispered stories, was alive in a way it hadn't been in years. Laughter rang through the cobbled streets, spilling from windows where candlelight flickered in the evenings.

Isla had taken up an old stone building in the heart of the village and turned it into an art studio, a place where she could create without restraint. Sunlight streamed through the large windows during the day, illuminating her work—the landscapes of the Highlands, the ever-changing moods of the loch, and portraits filled with stories only she could tell. Locals and travelers alike would stop by, drawn in by the warmth of the space, lingering to watch her paint or to purchase a piece of the land's beauty to take home with them.

Beside it, a small café had sprung to life, its doors always open, its tables always full. It had become a gathering place, a heart within the village. They served warm, crusty bread with fresh-churned butter, pastries that melted on the tongue, and, of course, the finest dishes crafted from the loch's bounty—fish caught by Callum himself in the early hours of the morning, alongside vegetables harvested from their own garden and those of their neighbors. It was a labor of love, woven together by the hands of the village, and it thrived because of it.

People had begun to come from out of town, drawn not only by the legend of the loch but by the warmth of the place itself. Some came for a day, some stayed longer, finding solace in the quiet beauty. The old cottage—Isla's cottage—had been lovingly restored, its walls now welcoming those who sought a retreat from the rush of the world. They had kept its charm intact, but with each board they mended, each stone they placed, it had become a gift—a sanctuary for those in need of one, just as it had once been for Isla.

Callum pressed a kiss to her temple, his other hand coming to rest gently over her belly. "I can't wait to meet them," he murmured, his voice rough with emotion.

Isla smiled, turning in his arms. "Neither can I." Her fingers brushed his jaw, tracing the familiar lines of the man who had once been a stranger but had become her home.

A breeze stirred around them, rustling the trees and sending a gentle ripple across the water. And in it, just for a moment, Isla swore she heard it—the last lingering note of the lullaby. Not a ghost, not a sorrowful echo, but a farewell. A blessing.

She closed her eyes, letting it settle in her bones, in her heart.

The past had been honored, the wounds had healed, and now—now, the future stretched before them, as boundless and full of promise as the horizon beyond the loch.

And with Callum's arms around her, with their child's heartbeat a steady rhythm in the quiet, she knew —

They were exactly where they were meant to be.

About the Author

Morgan is an author, entrepreneur, and homesteader living on their family farm in Manitoba, Canada with her husband, two children, and a variety of animals.

A retired veterinary technician, Morgan has transitioned into a creative life filled with farming, entrepreneurial ventures, and storytelling.

In addition to her romance novels, she has written Goat Keeping 101, The Art of Goat Milk Soap Making and is always working on more.

Morgan enjoys exploring creative outlets and finding inspiration in everyday moments. With lots more books in the works across various genres, Morgan is always seeking new ways to share stories and knowledge.

When she's not writing or running her business', she can be found spending time with her family, farming, or tending to her garden.